About t

Karen Warren was born during the Second World War in Denmark where she studied drama under Knud Hegelund at Skowlunde Theater and Danish literature at Horsholm college.

Karen's love of writing started as early as seven years old, whilst in the children's home where she lived from the ages of three to sixteen.

Karen has published several small pieces in various tabloids and poetry magazines both in England and abroad.

Karen moved to England, where she worked as a model with Irena Bentons Agency in Maddox Street, London.

After marrying a lawyer, and looking after her two children, Karen started working as a design consultant for overseas clients before divorcing and moving to France where she is now living.

Throughout her long life, Karen has never stopped writing though she has little time to deal with the commercial markets. She nevertheless, has completed twelve young children's books, two full novels, over two hundred fables, and a volume of spiritual writings.

Karen loves painting, reading all kinds of books, writing and enjoying seeing her friends at her home.

This is a work of fiction. Names, characters, businesses, places, events and incidents are either the products of the author's imagination or used in a fictitious manner. Any resemblance to actual persons, living or dead, or actual events is purely coincidental.

To Duke & Dada —
Much Love

Karen Crist

GRACE
FROM HEAVEN TO HELL ON EARTH

K M ROAN

GRACE
FROM HEAVEN TO HELL ON EARTH

Vanguard Press

VANGUARD PAPERBACK

© Copyright 2022
K M Roan

The right of K M Roan to be identified as author of
this work has been asserted by her in accordance with the
Copyright, Designs and Patents Act 1988.

All Rights Reserved

No reproduction, copy or transmission of this publication
may be made without written permission.
No paragraph of this publication may be reproduced,
copied or transmitted save with the written permission of the
publisher, or in accordance with the provisions
of the Copyright Act 1956 (as amended).

Any person who commits any unauthorised act in relation to
this publication may be liable to criminal
prosecution and civil claims for damages.

A CIP catalogue record for this title is

available from the British Library.

ISBN 978 1 80016 350 8

*Vanguard Press is an imprint of
Pegasus Elliot MacKenzie Publishers Ltd.*
www.pegasuspublishers.com

First Published in 2022

Vanguard Press
Sheraton House Castle Park
Cambridge England

Printed & Bound in Great Britain

Dedication

To my friends and family for their love and support.

Chapter 1

As I lay waiting to be born, the Angel of Life brought my Earthly clothes, a tight-fitting mantle of pale golden skin, with which he covered me from head to toe.

"A perfect fit." The angel stretched himself to his full height of eight feet and then gave a satisfied smile that lit up the space around us. "How does it feel?" He stretched out his finger to straighten the loose skin around my neck.

I kicked my legs and wriggled my toes. "Soft and smooth." I gave a toothless yawn as I tried to turn around the best I could in my confined space.

"Clever girl." The angel laughed with a deep rumbling sound at my clumsy attempt. "Come," he said, taking hold of my hand, "we still have a lot to do before you are born."

He helped me to my feet, then hand-in-hand, we walked away from my tight space into a large room opening up in front of us, where a magnificent ivory coloured chest of drawers was hanging from above by silver chains.

The Angel opened the top drawer where a million orbs in all colours and sizes lay looking at themselves.

He searched amongst them before picking up a pair of deep sapphire blue. He held them in front of me.

"Now, what do you think of these?"

I sensed the orbs looking at me. "What are they for?" I asked curiously.

"They are called eyes, and they are what you need to see with once you are born." The angel gently placed the eyes on either side of my upturned nose, making me blink so rapidly that tears ran down my cheeks.

"Excellent." He smiled. "Now that they are fitted and washed, they should last you for a lifetime."

He clapped his hands loudly three times, and a star-covered cloth appeared from out of nowhere. The angel dried my tears with the cloth and then picked two of the smallest stars, placing one in each of my eyes, making them shine and sparkle.

"You will also need something to hear with on Earth." The angel opened a second drawer and took out a pair of tiny pink ears, which he blew into before moulding them to the side of my head.

Suddenly I began to hear different sounds that were so strange I tried to pull the ears off again.

"What have you done to me?" I asked, panic-stricken.

The angel gave me a reassuring hug. "I have cleared the channels between the inner ears and your brain. So that you will have perfect hearing after birth." He then adjusted one of the ears by turning it slightly to the left.

"Why? Why do I need anything different when I can see and hear perfectly well?"

"You don't need anything different." The angel waved his hands, making two white turtle doves fly down from their golden perch to remove the chest of drawers. "You need something additional." He wiped his hands on his flowing white robe. "Something called the five human senses. You will learn all about them in time."

I did not understand.

"What you are seeing and hearing with now are your inner senses which will be our connection with you on Earth. Don't worry your head about any of that now." He plucked a feather from his mighty wings and tickled my chin, making me sneeze so violently that it straightened my upturned nose.

He smiled at my surprised look. "That is better; now you are perfect!" He replaced the feather and then shook his wings furiously, causing a two-way mirror to fall from the branch of a huge tree that spread its crown of knowledge above us.

"Take a look." The angel held the mirror in front of me, and there I saw a small girl with long, dark hair, a pert little nose, button mouth and sapphire eyes set well apart.

"Is that me in there?" I looked curiously at the image before it faded and disappeared.

The angel wiped the mirror clean. "Yes. That is what you will look like as a young girl. But you will change with the years and in time, will turn into this." He held the reverse side of the mirror in front of me.

I watched, fascinated, as the little girl began to change from a child into a young woman, then into maturity, before fading into an old woman with wrinkled skin and pale eyes and hair.

"Oh, no! What has happened to me?" I touched my face to make sure I was still myself.

"That's what is called the circle of life, another thing you will learn about on Earth." He hung the mirror back on the branch of the tree, which bent its crown towards me, bidding me to taste its fruit.

Timidly, I plucked a handful of the strange-looking fruits and quickly swallowed them. Immediately, I felt my head swelling with a new understanding.

I wonder what is going to happen to me on Earth? I looked around me with my new eyes but, as yet, could see nothing with them.

With an unsure voice, I asked the angel, "Will my life on Earth be a happy one?"

The angel looked at me with gentle eyes. "Happiness depends on how you use the gifts you bring with you to Earth."

"Gifts?" I rubbed my eyes and looked around me again. "Where?"

"Come with me. I will show you a room full of Earthly treasures where you can make your choice."

A vast door opened in front of us and a huge banner, bearing the words Earthly Treasures stretched across the room.

There were caskets of gold and silver pushing each other aside so as to be better admired, and velvet boxes parted their bright red lips to show their priceless jewels within. Precious pearls rolled with tremendous speed across the white marble floor, smoothing any rough edges of imperfection and, above, glittering crystals hung in spectacular profusion from every corner of the room.

Below, discarded angels' wings were busily stirring the delicious food cooking in emerald pots.

I stepped further into the room, which rang with the merry laughter of people who danced, while others were drinking from crystal goblets or making love behind a gossamer wall. Musical masterpieces were being played on all the instruments of the world, and fine artistic works, rarely seen outside Heaven, were painting themselves.

High on a scaffold stood an old angel, his lined face caked with splashes of paint. He took no notice of me, being too busy painting tomorrow's inventions. I watched, fascinated, as he named each one with a rapid finger stroke.

"A million years of invention should be enough for the scientists to get on with," he muttered to himself, wiping his brow with a complicated mathematical formula. The platform he worked from swerved like ocean waves, ebbing and flowing with each brush stroke.

Suddenly, he turned around and caught me staring at him. He smiled in recognition though I had never seen him before. I smiled back. The old painter raised his wet brush and drips of paint fell on me, also splashing the floor. As I licked the sweet-tasting paint from my fingers, a kaleidoscope of words began to spin around in my head as a new power took hold of me.

Bewildered by so many wonderful things, I asked the Angel of Life, who had stood quietly by my side, to help me choose my gift.

"No. That is not possible," he said. "The choice must be yours alone. Take your time and look around." He dragged a chair from one of the newly painted canvases leaning against the wall and sat down, but not before he had dried it with his hot breath.

"I want music!" I laughed, trying to catch the notes that danced as tinkling bells near my ears. "No, wait… perhaps the paintings would be better?" I dipped my fingers into the sticky substance and then watched as it was transformed into beautiful shapes.

Suddenly, I heard the most exquisite words being recited. I ran towards the sound, and there in front of me, was a classroom full of souls, writing the living words on long scrolls of paper, yellow with age. At the head of the class stood an old wizardly soul, dictating.

"You have to be quick to hear what I say." His mouth opened wide, releasing a stream of words that, once written, belonged to everyone.

"I want some of those living words!" I shouted, hardly able to control myself. "For with them I can create images as real as paintings and make music as powerful as any that can be played on an instrument."

The old soul's face turned towards me. "Hold out your hands, child," he ordered.

I did as he asked, and as the words poured from his mouth, I caught as many of the letters as I could and carefully placed them under my tunic. My heart sang with joy as I ran towards the exit.

The Angel of Life stood up and looked at me with loving eyes, pointing to my bulging tunic. "You have made your choice?"

"Yes. Let's go." I couldn't wait to start using them.

"Come, we still have time before your birth." He glanced at the universal clock that hung on a beam of light above our heads and then shook himself vigorously, creating a strong current of cool air around us. I shivered so much that I almost dropped my precious collection of letters.

"There are two more rooms I must show you… come." The entrance door to the universal treasures closed silently behind us, and I followed the angel as he walked towards the very centre of the universe where stars were performing their final dance and the moon hung upside down, showing its naked side.

After walking only a short distance, we stopped in front of a slimy, green, fungus covered wall. It stretched to all corners of the world, although it seemed no distance from where we stood. From an old rusty nail hung a key that exuded as much evil as a poisonous snake. The key spat fire and black fumes rose like a tail from the other end.

The Angel of Life put on protective gloves before taking hold of the key and turning it to the right three times. A huge black door slowly swung open, creaking fearfully. He stepped aside, allowing me to see what lay beyond, and there I saw an emptiness so vast that it made me feel as if all life had drained out of me.

Trembling with fear of the unknown, I asked the angel, "Why do I feel this way just by looking into that?" I pointed to the void in front of me.

The angel carefully removed the gloves, which instantly disappeared behind a passing grey cloud before he answered me.

"That is what your life on Earth will feel like if you fail to develop your chosen gift."

With a loud moaning noise, the great door began to close and then, with a mighty bang, shut tight behind us. The key turned itself three times to the left and, with the wall, disappeared.

Uncertain of my ability to develop my chosen gift, I thought it would perhaps be wiser to have a few others to fall back on. Discomfited, I shifted my weight from one foot to the other. The angel began walking ahead of me so quickly that I had to run to catch him up.

"How much can I take with me from the room of universal treasures?" I asked, gasping for breath.

No sooner had the question left my lips than a strange feeling of greed came from nowhere, wrapping itself tightly around me so that the letters hidden beneath my tunic were completely scrambled before being flattened insensibly against my naked body.

"As much as you like." The angel's eyes, now like piercing lights, held a question. When he spoke again, his voice had changed to a deep rumble. "But remember that everything you see there may not be what it appears to be." As if he could read my thoughts, he continued, now speaking in a lighter voice and enunciating each word. "But if you choose your gift with love and wisdom, it cannot fail, with determination and hard work, to make your life rich and meaningful."

Still unsure, I asked quietly how I would know whether I had chosen wisely.

"Perhaps the living words are only illusions?" My voice could hardly be heard above the great roar that rose like a black mist from the reappearing slimy wall. The emptiness seeped through the wall like a slow-moving purple spring. The roar continued, varying in pitch from a high, screeching sound to a deep, mellow rumble. With each roar, the wall shook so violently that I feared for my life. I quickly stepped as far back from it as I could.

The angel, who had stood calmly beside me, now stepped protectively in front of me and raised his sight towards a dark green form that was gradually unfolding itself into a huge tree with rose-coloured leaves. Strangely, the shadows of the leaves formed a bright ring of light.

The angel reached towards the light, pulling from it a golden ring that he tightly knotted around my heart.

"What does your heart tell you?" he asked.

With renewed certainty, I replied, "It tells me that I want my life to be filled with beauty and love."

As soon as I had uttered those words, the roaring sound from the room of emptiness ceased, and the hand of greed released its grip on my heart. I felt as if I were born anew.

"Whenever someone is about to be born," the angel said, "I show them that room so that they might understand the difference that emptiness can make to their lives. But you are trembling; come, let me show you something heart-warming... your Earth family." He smiled at my hesitation, then lifted me into his arms. His protective warmth quickly calmed my jittery nerves as he walked with long, sure strides towards a grand staircase, rising like a tower towards the centre of the universe. He climbed to the top of the stairs and then stopped in front of a small, round window supported by two strong pillars.

He pointed with a long, pale finger. "Look through there."

Curiously, I peeped through the rose-coloured glass and looked out onto a lush green meadow where two red cows meandered side by side. To the left, a young, dark-haired man was hard at work sawing logs. He paused to wave to a beautiful auburn-haired woman who was coming out of a small whitewashed cottage, around which a profusion of flowers danced in the breeze.

In one hand she held a plate of cakes; with the other she rubbed her protruding abdomen. The man shouted something to her. She grimaced as she shouted back.

He threw down his saw and then raised his face towards me. For a split second we looked into each other's eyes. A fire of love like a burning river ran through my whole being. I closed my eyes, savouring the feeling before looking out again.

The man ran towards the woman, hugging her with strong arms before leading her back inside the cottage.

Pointing to the scene below the window, I turned my face to the angel, who still held me. "Is that where I will live on Earth?"

"Yes, that beautiful place, filled with love, warmth and friendship, will be the place of your birth and seeing that love all around you will help you to develop your own gift."

With a smile, he patted my tunic, where the letters now lay dormant. "However, life on Earth is never just one thing," he said, shaking his head. He set me down and took hold of my hand before continuing. "There will be hard times as well as beautiful moments. You will encounter tears as well as laughter, but you will always, because of your chosen gift, be in touch with us to obtain guidance for your own development. It all takes time; the pregnant woman you saw just now carries her child for nine months before birth.

"Everything in life has its time for developing and growing before ending its season. You will discover that for yourself as a young child when you will be waiting impatiently for the apples to ripen in the orchard and flowers to emerge from the dark Earth. Nature's laws are all the same, whatever form it takes.

"Everything in life has its own gift; that is the marvel of creation. If you are ever in doubt, just study the laws of nature, and you will soon understand and be guided by your soul; that is your gift from the Creator himself."

"Can I live without my soul?" I queried.

The angel's eyes were as deep as a forest pool, and he seemed to look right through me as he replied. "You will be alive, but as for living… that is something you will have to discover for yourself. I will show you another room where humans who believed they could live without their souls are now recovering."

The next chamber we entered was lit by a single bulb suspended from the ceiling by a hangman's loop. Everything within the room was in disarray. Chairs and tables were upside down, some with legs broken off, and the air was polluted and foul, reeking of stale food mixed with the stench of humans.

But worst of all was the wailing and crying of the strange entities who crouched close to the floor, clawing at each other. They looked so horrific and dangerous as they fought for justice that I clung tightly to the angel with one hand while I held the other over my letters, fearful that they may be damaged.

The angel closed the door. He pointed to the room. "It is sad," he said, "but all is not lost. After some time, these souls will attend the Old Father of Wisdom's class, where they will be helped to change their visions so that they will see clearly where they went wrong. In the meantime, they must live, as you saw, within the room of their mistakes.

"But time is moving on. You will soon have to go through the chambers of change, but first let me take you to meet the Old Father of Wisdom."

The Old Father of Wisdom stood before us. His long white beard reached from here to eternity, and all the wisdom of the world and beyond was woven into the strands of his hair. His eyes were of a colour not unlike gold and shone with equal power.

"You have chosen your gift?" he asked, eyeing my hands that nervously fingered the front of my tunic. "You will also have been told how to use it wisely." His voice roared like thunder, prompting lightning sparks to shoot out of his mouth.

With a terrible fear, I remembered the vast empty room and the chamber with the lost souls.

"Yes," I whispered.

"Now tell me how you will use your gift," he commanded.

I closed my eyes and again saw in front of me the harmonious setting of the little whitewashed cottage surrounded by flowers and lush, green fields.

"To bring beauty and love into the world," I answered quickly.

"You have chosen well." The Old Father touched my head with a hand as light as a feather. "You are already absorbing the living spirit and, as you have chosen only one gift, you should be able to achieve your goal… with a little help, that is. Most souls who go to the room of Earthly treasures take so much with them that, sadly, they will never be able to sort it all out in a lifetime, and therefore, will be unable to use their gifts to their full potential.

"But never forget that your gift came from a room full of Earthly vices. These vices will also be part of you… learn to recognise them. Do not let them destroy the fragile flame of your gift, for they are jealous, and jealousy will have a powerful influence on your Earthly stay.

"Again, I emphasise, use your gift wisely, and the power of the living spirit within your letters will fill your soul with a glorious light so strong that you will have no choice but to follow wherever it takes you. And also know this: that light will transform not only your life, but also the lives of everyone it comes into contact with, bringing beauty into people's lives and filling their hearts with love."

The Old Father of Wisdom looked into my eyes. "You will be called Grace," he said, "as Grace in body, spirit and soul."

I thanked the Master as he turned around to leave and then walked slowly to the stairs that were to take me to the Earth below.

"Please," I begged the angel, "is it too late to give you back my gift?" Suddenly I felt afraid of all the mistakes I could make with it.

"It is too late. You have chosen it, and now you must go. But fear not; I will be your helper and companion at all times." He gently touched my head with the flame of life, and then he was gone.

With trembling hands, I held on to my precious letters. "Be my friend, not my enemy," I whispered as I placed one cautious foot on the stairway leading down to the Earth.

Chapter 2

As I proceeded down the stairs, I met others like myself, trembling, taking a step at a time, clutching their gifts tightly.

"I am called the Führer!" one dark soul shouted in a voice so loud that the force nearly knocked me over. He dragged behind him a black sack, bearing the word Power in crimson letters.

"What's in your bag?" I asked timidly.

He squinted at me with a sly eye. "Evil, hatred, greed and money." He grinned, showing a mouth full of rotting teeth.

Surprised, I asked, "Why so many horrible things?"

"They are what I need to give me this." He pointed to his bag with the bright red letters that began running like a fast-flowing river of blood, down the stairs.

I quickly skipped aside, out of their way. "Did the Old Father of Wisdom not warn you about these vices?" I was gripped by an icy fear as he reached out to touch me.

"I never saw…" He looked puzzled. "Who is he? The only one I saw was a blond youth who tripped me up as the Angel of Life walked me past the chamber of lost souls, where he was hiding." He narrowed his sly eyes at me and hissed, "Take me with you, and I will give you a power that has never been seen on Earth before. With such power, you will have need of neither God nor man."

With those words, he pushed my soul aside and then took its place next to my heart, telling me where to find the things I would need to take with me to Earth.

"I will be world-famous!" the Führer shouted even louder as he ran past me. "Out of the way! I'd better get down there and start my life before you arrive, as it seems to me that you have precious little to bring with you…" his voice faded as he disappeared from view.

Another soul I met had musical notes hanging from his ears. In his hand, he carried the double-edged sword of composition like a baton.

"With my sword I shall cut down everything that stands in my way of composing," he sang in a beautiful soprano voice. "For I want to be heard and when I am, I shall command huge sums from kings and peasants alike." He flourished his sword above his head, singing, "I am ready for my work… I am ready for my work."

"But what about those?" I asked, pointing to the notes hanging from his ears.

"Here, have one." He threw me a tiny note. "And remember me when you hear it." He blew on the note, which instantly began to play a joyous tune that made me want to sing and dance at the same time.

"That is the music from Debussy's *Jardins Sous La Pluie*." He laughed. "Music is going to be my price."

"Your price? Price for what?"

"Fame, of course. Don't you know anything?" He waved his hand. "Farewell, my friend. We will meet again, no doubt." He blew me a kiss before the notes carried him away.

"No doubt," I called to his receding form as I fastened the note to my ear.

Then I saw a dark female form, hiding beneath a large black cloak with a multi-coloured lining. In her hand were the living colours I had seen in the room of Earthly treasures.

"I borrowed these," she whispered. "They are old, but I am going to use them to paint new images. I shall hide myself with them under my cloak until they become so alive that the whole world will want to share them with me... only then will I have the courage to show my true self. I will be recognised by the magic of my colours, but for years before that, I will live a life of loneliness and fear; some will even say emptiness, but only because they won't have understood about my life."

"Loneliness and fear seem a terrible price to pay," I told her. "Couldn't you be recognised without that?"

She shook her head, and in a girlish voice, said, "I wouldn't know. Darkness threw her cloak over me and told me I would always have her to keep me warm and safe. She felt so strong and protective, and now I don't dare move without it, though I can't see clearly from beneath it, and it weighs me down so much that I can hardly straighten my back." She paused, and I saw her head tilt to one side. "Do you want to share it with me?"

I told her I had no need of it, but offered to carry some of the colours that filled both her hands.

She gave me a handful. They felt like living embryos as they twisted and wriggled between my fingers. I looked at them with longing.

"What marvellous colours, I wish I had some."

Her bright eyes peeped out briefly. "Keep them," she said before retreating even further into her cloak.

We were getting closer to Earth now. A stream of cold air wrapped itself around me, making me shiver, and for a moment, I wished I had taken up the offer of sharing her cloak.

A young woman walked towards me, carrying two small children in her arms.

"Could you help me?" She sounded totally exhausted. "They were left behind on the stairs." She smiled at the children. "I am premature and must return." She held out the children towards me.

The children and I looked at each other. They were beautiful. I stretched out my arms towards them.

"Come with me, I will look after you." I snuggled the children safely under my tunic, where I could feel their tiny hearts beating against mine.

Then they spied the colours I was still carrying in my hands. "May we play with them?" they pleaded.

"I would love to share them with you." I gave them a small handful each, and they carefully crept out from beneath my tunic and immediately started to paint the treads of the stairs as we walked down.

When I looked disapprovingly at them, they just laughed, and the sound was like that of tiny silver bells. They pointed at the brightly coloured stairway.

"Now we have left something of us behind that will last forever."

I looked behind me; it was beautiful. "You are clever children," I told them. "Let us hope that others will appreciate it as well."

A thin young man, whose flowing black hair danced in the gentle breeze, followed us down and caught up with us.

He looked at me with sparkling grey eyes. "Have you a place to stay on Earth?" he asked politely.

"I don't know," I replied, equally politely, for by now, the memory of my Earth family had faded into the subconscious.

As the developing consciousness extended into the here and now, he winked. "Well then, come with me? I will look after you."

He stepped in front of me and without another thought, I began to follow him.

He looked back at the children and me, with a grin. "I like what you are carrying," he said, pointing to the children who were now sleeping like two small doves in my arms. He bent forward to kiss them.

Suddenly, I noticed a mass of grey matter like a slimy river trailing behind him.

"What is that?" I asked, pointing to the mass as it began running between our legs.

"Deceit." He laughed loudly. "Don't pay any attention to that." He had changed his voice so that he sounded gracious and charming.

Be aware of his vices... I could hear the stern voice of the Old Father of Wisdom speaking from within my heart, and I stopped immediately.

"I'm sorry, but I won't be able to walk with you any further. I need to be on my own." I did not know what else to say.

The young man stopped, giving me a look of surprise. He bowed courteously. "As you wish," he said, in an indifferent tone,. "But as we are both going the same way, at least let me carry the children for you." He reached out to take them. "Remember, however, that no one is perfect," he said arrogantly. "Least of all you, as you will no doubt discover for yourself."

"Can we keep the colours?" the children shouted.

With tears in my eyes, it was all I could do to nod my head as I tried to ignore the sting of his words and watched as he gathered them in his arms and walked away with Deceit trailing after him down towards Earth.

"We will meet again," he called, waving a hand. "I will be called a Charmer, and you are Grace." He laughed. "I will remember you!"

"We will meet again," the children echoed, waving their own farewell with small, paint-stained hands, like colourful butterflies.

I waved back until they were out of sight.

Suddenly, a small brown fawn danced in front of me.

"I am not really a fawn," it said, "but no one knows except me. I wanted to take intellect with me to Earth, but it was too heavy for me to carry, so I changed into a fawn. I will always remain a kid, but my intellect will show above all else."

I was curious. "Will you be happy with so much intellect?"

"I think so." It stretched its long legs in front of me. "I have heard that there is a great demand for it on Earth."

"Not having any of it myself," I answered sadly, "I wonder what it will be like?"

The fawn licked my hand with its rough tongue. "As I can't give it to you, be my friend and then we can share it."

"Thank you." I stroked its silky coat. "There are so many things I need to learn about… perhaps I will also discover intellect."

The fawn nodded. "Well, so long," it said, leaping away. "Until then."

"Until then." I blew it a kiss.

Then a shower of green apples came tumbling down around me. I picked one up and bit into it.

"Don't do that!" an angry voice shrieked.

Startled, I dropped the apple. "You can talk?"

"Of course I can talk," the apple replied indignantly. "But I am always misunderstood. Everyone thinks I am an apple. It really hurts when I am bitten into, you know."

"Sorry. But what are you?" I couldn't keep the surprise out of my voice.

"Can't you see?" The apple pointed to itself, moving its leaf up and down.

As hard as I tried, I could see nothing but an apple.

When I didn't answer, the apple continued. "Don't tell me you can't see me, either," it sneered.

Something about its tone scared me, and I began to walk away.

"Wait!" the apple shouted. "Don't go yet. I want to know what you are hiding." It pointed to the bulge in my tunic. "And what's that?" it asked, touching the paint smears on my hands. "Ugh! It's wet!" Trying to wipe off the paint with its green leaf, it then spotted the note hanging from my ear. "And what, pray, is that?"

I explained what it was, and also that I was carrying living letters under my tunic.

"Whatever for?"

"To make beautiful words with."

"What for?" The apple rolled in front of me.

"So that I might give people on Earth something beautiful from myself." I tried to step over the apple as it continued rolling at my feet.

"But you are beautiful to look at. Isn't that enough?"

"No…" I hesitated, trying to find the right words. "Long after my beauty fades, my letters will still be shining."

"May I see some of them?" The apple turned its bright red underside towards me.

I fished out a few tiny letters; they wriggled like worms in my hand.

"Let me hold them." Without warning, the apple snatched the letters from my hand. "I will keep these." It laughed, and started to roll swiftly away from me.

"No! Give them back!" I cried in despair. "They are my gift."

The apple gathered speed, ignoring my plea.

"If you steal, you will have a terrible price to pay and one day I will find you and make you give them back to me," I shouted as I caught up with it and gave it a good hard kick.

"Ouch! Don't do that, it hurts."

I gave it another, even harder kick.

The apple quickly swallowed the letters as it tried to escape from me.

"I can understand why no one recognises you," I told it. "For you are indeed in disguise, but I will recognise you by the letters you have stolen." My anger was such that I could hardly speak, and I then gave it one final kick which sent it spinning down the stairs at great speed.

Exhausted and unhappy, I sat down on the step, unable to go any further. My anger felt like a black vapour surrounding me, making it impossible for me to see.

The Angel of Light came down to lift the anger away and then called on Forgiveness, so that I might be acquainted with her gentle face before continuing my journey.

Darkness started to disperse as I walked towards the light, but not before securing the letters within my heart. That way I would always have them with me wherever I went and whatever I was doing.

Chapter 3
(Eight years later)

On a grey autumn afternoon in Ham, three young children, a boy and two girls, ran like the wind down a narrow muddy lane leading from the small hamlet situated between Kingston upon Thames and Richmond, Surrey. It looked as if the tall, dark-haired boy was chasing the two youngsters. One of the girls, a pale, delicate child with a long, blonde ponytail, was almost out of breath. She struggled to keep up with the slightly younger girl, whose dark pigtails whipped across her face as she ran ahead with long strides. Suddenly she stopped and turned around, nearly colliding with the girl running close behind her.

Her eyes blazing, she raised her hand and pointed towards the boy, who had also stopped, and yelled as loud as she could, "Well… we-e-e-e… have a Bugatti." Seven-year-old Grace stuck her tongue out at Frederic. "So *there!*"

Frederic stood with his hand raised, ready to hit her. "What is that?" His voice held a tone of… *I don't believe you, stupid… whatever it is…* "My mum says that you are as poor as a church mouse," he shouted. "And the only things *you* have, are lice and fleas. And our dad says we are *not* to play with you. Come, Jane." He turned towards his little sister, who stood behind him. "Come on!" He slapped her hard on the back before sticking his tongue out at Grace, who stood with her head bent, trying not to cry.

"And *my* dad says it is not true that you were born feet first, you little liar. It is only *something* you are making up, *just* to make yourself *more* interesting!" he shouted at the top of his voice. "Move!" he slapped Jane's arm. "Don't stand there looking at that *stupid* girl."

Jane stumbled forward, then turned her head and smiled at Grace, as Frederic pulled her around.

Grace smiled tearfully back, then wiped her nose with the end of her long black pigtail, before shouting, "It is *too*... you are just a stupid boy who doesn't know anything!"

"Who are *you* calling stupid?" Frederic's ice-blue eyes flashed dangerously as he slowly walked back and then gave her a hard push that sent her flying.

"Ahhhh!" Grace screamed as she landed in a small muddy pool. "Now look what you have done, you *stupid* boy. My mother will *kill* you."

Grace stood up, as muddy water dripped from her dress, down her legs, and into her black strappy shoes.

"It is my best Sunday dress. My dad will *get* you for this." Grace rubbed her bruised knees, then wiped her tear-stained face with a muddy hand.

"Yaaah! Just let him try." Frederic screwed his face up.

"My dad says, your dad is nothing but a lazy layabout, and a dreamer who doesn't work. And your mother has to bake bread to sell at the bakery, just to feed you."

Frederic was outraged. "My dad says, that your dad will never amount to *anything*. He has no principles and should never have had you, *stupid girl*, if he cannot afford to look after you — *so there*!" He turned and started to walk back to where Jane stood with tearful eyes and her mouth open, waiting to see what would happen next.

"He can, too... look after us!" Grace shouted to Frederic's back. "He sold an article to *The Times* last week, and they are sending him a cheque. And my mother bakes bread because she likes it, not like yours, who never goes into the kitchen. And your stuck-up father rides around on that fat horse of his, looking like he owns the town, just because he is the mayor. My father," continued Grace, as she tried to brush the mud off her dress, "says he is a pompous ass, with no more sense between his ears than a rat has between his legs. And I hate you," she spat. "You are a fat stupid boy, and how you got a lovely sister like Jane, I will never know. My father says she must have been a foundling. She is so different, being blonde, while you and your parents all have black hair. So there!"

Frederic had turned and advanced again. "I will teach you," he hissed, as he grabbed hold of one of Grace's pigtails and gave it a severe pull.

"Auk... ouch... let go!" She punched his arm. "Let go, I tell you... ooh... ouch!"

"And take that, too." Frederic pulled Grace's pale green ribbon off and trampled it down in the dirt, then quickly ran back, taking his sister's hand. "Come, Jane, let's go. And don't ever play with that lousy girl again."

"But I like her, Frederic. She's my friend." Eight-year-old Jane looked up at her brother, with large green eyes set in a small oval face. Her mane of golden hair was tied back in a ponytail with bright red ribbon.

"I am telling you, Jane," he hissed, "Mum won't have you playing with that madam." Twelve-year-old Frederic jerked a thumb over his shoulder in the direction of Grace. "She is full of fantasies and lies. Feet first, indeed. The little liar," he mumbled. "Anyone knows that the head pops out first when you are born. Grace is always trying to make herself more interesting than she is... don't ever believe her again! She doesn't even have another dress; she always wears the same one." Frederic nodded his head. "Poor, wretched girl!"

"Yes, I know," Jane whispered. "But she told me that her mother washes and presses it every night, ready for her to wear the next day. That is almost like having a new one."

Jane looked down at her own blue-and-white dress, and wished her mother would wash it every day, as she always managed to spill something on it. But her mother would never dream of washing anything; she left all that to Clara, the cleaner, and she only came once a week. And Mary, the old cook, had enough to do in the kitchen, as well as looking after the house, without having to do the laundry as well.

Jane turned her head and looked back to where Grace stood wiping the mud off her dress. She waved her hand and smiled. Grace looked tearfully back at her, before running home to the little cottage standing well hidden from the road, in a green field.

Next to the gatepost stood an old oak tree, spreading its crown. Halfway up, between the crossed branches, Grace and her father had started to build a treehouse. Her father had written a sign saying, Hidden Cottage, with an arrow pointing upwards, then hammered it to the tree.

As Grace opened the gate, she disturbed some sparrows feeding on crumbs her mother had thrown out for them. With a flutter of wings, they flew away as she walked towards her mother, a slim, beautiful woman with long auburn hair who stood in the open doorway, wiping her floury hands on her white apron.

"Good God, child! What has happened to you?" Her mother looked at her, horrified. "Just look at your dress? And where is your hair ribbon?"

Grace handed her the dirty ribbon, and began telling her the story as her mother hurried her inside and closed the door, before taking her daughter upstairs to her bedroom, where she helped her undress.

"Take your shoes and socks off; I will have to clean them for you." Anna took off her cardigan and held it out. "Here, put this on, it should be long enough to cover you up until your dress is washed and dry."

Anna went over to switch the electric heater on, opened out a clothes airer in front of it and then went to the corner sink and began washing.

"You poor thing," she said, as Grace finished with her story. "Frederic again! That boy needs a clip round the ear. There is no end to his mischief... how he could ever have dear little Jane as a sister is beyond me. Such a darling child; I do hope she will come and see us again."

"I don't know, Mum. Frederic told me that their parents don't want her to because we are poor and because they think I have lice and fleas."

"Such nonsense." Anna turned her face away from the steam of the hot water. "Where do those stories come from? I am sure it is only something Frederic has made up. We have always got on well with his parents." Irritated, she wiped her forehead with her arm.

Grace pulled her mother's yellow cardigan over her head, and then started to roll the sleeves up. "There's a hole in it, Mum." She poked her finger through it.

"I know." Her mother sighed. "I do love that old cardigan, and it is falling to pieces. I will have to try and mend it the best I can."

Grace wriggled her finger in the hole. "Are we really as poor as Frederic says, Mum?" Grace sat down on her bed and began swinging her legs to and fro.

Anna stopped washing and looked at her. "My dear little girl, yes, we are poor, very poor, but that has never been a crime. Many people are in the same position, especially so soon after the war. But you don't have, and have never had, any lice and fleas, that is pure imagination on behalf of that spiteful boy. I've a good mind to go and tell his parents what he has done to you."

"Don't, Mum. Please. I'm all right."

"But how did it all start?" Anna's voice came through the hot steam from the sink. "What did you do to provoke him?" She pushed a stray lock of auburn hair behind her ear.

"I didn't do anything." Grace picked up her favourite toy rabbit and put it under the cardigan.

"I only told him I was born feet first, and then he called me a liar. But it is true, you told me so. And Daddy wrote a poem about it. And… only nobody wanted to buy it, so he tore it up. And now I don't remember how it went."

"I do." Her mother laughed. "But it wasn't a poem, just a jingle."

"A jingle? What is that?"

"A jingle is a short musical verse, or set of verses, often used to advertise a product."

"I see. Like advertising that I was born?"

"You could say that. Anyway, this is how it went." Anna dried her hands and then sat down next to Grace on the bed and began singing.

"Ten pink toes Oh! Oh! Oh!
Curiously, came feet first into this world,
Wriggling away, as if to say
Hallo, Mum and Dad, we are here to stay.

But wait, there is more to see.
Two tiny hands,
A belly round and sweet
And then, finally,
The beautiful head of
Our darling Grace."

Grace laughed, together with her mother.

Back at the sink, Anna turned towards her daughter. "You know, Grace, I can't help thinking that you must have said something else to provoke Frederic?" Her searching look said, come on now, you'd better tell me everything.

Grace's cheeks coloured slightly as she looked down.

Her mother stopped washing. "I thought as much. Now let me hear exactly what went on. What did you say to him, madam?"

"I told him that his father had no more sense between his ears than a rat has between its legs, and that we have a Bugatti."

"Good God, child! Whatever made you say something as vulgar as that? And to say that we have a Bugatti… that is a deliberate lie. You know that is not true."

"It is. We do have one! Dad showed it to me in his workshop. And I only said what I did about his father, because he called Dad a good-for-nothing layabout."

"Grace, the car is only a model your father bought as a kind of status symbol, to show us that one day he will make enough money to buy one of the most expensive cars in the world."

"I know, Mum. But I was not lying. We do have one, but I didn't tell him how big it is."

"Grace, you know that is called lying by omission, and you are old enough to know that life does not depend on the material wealth we have, but on our goodness and strength to face everything we have to deal with. Next time you see Jane, will you please tell her the whole truth? Promise?"

Grace nodded. Her mother lifted her chin up and looked into her eyes. "Promise?" she repeated.

"Sorry, Mum. Yes, I promise."

"Good."

Anna went over to place the clothes on the airer and then sat wearily on the bed again.

"Grace, Grace." She shook her head. "You must learn to stand tall, in spite of life's adversities. Now, what are we going to do whilst your clothes dry? You can't go out like that." She stood up and tied Grace's hair back where it had come loose.

"Let's go down to the lounge and find some writing paper and perhaps you could write a letter to Jane, to say how sorry you are about today? And Miss Grey, your English teacher, tells me how well you are doing except that you must pay more attention to your grammar, so why don't you practice that as well?"

Grace slid off her bed and hugged her mum. "I love you, and I don't care if we are poor, as long as I have you and Dad."

"Neither do I." Her mother laughed. "As long as I have you, you little monkey! Come now, let's get on with more light-hearted matters."

"You know, Mum, I don't really hate Frederic, but he is a prat. Why does he always get at me?"

Anna sat down on the bed again.

"Sit down, Grace." She put her arms around her. "Frederic is going through a difficult stage in his life. He is nearly thirteen years old, a teenager, and his body is going through lots of changes, which at times make him difficult to be with. Frederic is also highly sensitive, which shows in his excellent piano playing. I believe he has won a scholarship to Westminster in London, where he is to study music. So he will soon be leaving here. I can assure you that it is not easy for him to suddenly find himself with feelings and emotions he doesn't know how to handle. It is all part of growing up, and you must learn to be more tolerant when dealing with him. It can be a very disturbing period. Hopefully, he will soon grow out of it."

"Like I grow out of my old clothes and have to have new ones?"

"No, not quite." Her mother smiled. "He is not getting anything new, but developing something that is already part of him. Like an apple tree, when a beautiful blossom grows into a sweet-tasting apple."

Grace clapped her hands. "I know, and like the flowers that grow from the earth."

"Exactly, you are a very perceptive girl."

"Hopefully, he will become a sweet apple, not like the sour ones on Farmer Jones's tree. No one wants them."

Her mother laughed. "I hope so, too. We will just have to wait and see. In the meantime, young lady, let us get on with your work."

Grace jumped down from the bed and took her mother's rough hand, looking up at her with wide sapphire eyes, full of love. "I am so lucky to have you to love me."

"We are both lucky, and never forget it." Her mother smiled.

"I won't, Mum, and in future, I will try not to tell fibs."

"Do that, love, and learn to be patient with that which can be difficult to deal with." Her mother stroked Grace's chin.

"Aw! Your nail is broken, Mum. It's scratching me."

"Sorry, dear, I caught it on the cheese grater when I grated the carrots for our salad this afternoon."

"So we will have carrots with a nail dressing tonight?" Grace giggled.

"Oh! You silly…" Anna slapped her behind gently.

"Where's Dad, Mum?"

"He is down in the garden shed, working on another long poem about the brave soldiers going off to war, bringing back such bitter memories with their victory. For regardless which side you are on and how victorious, it is always with a sense of loss."

Grace looked a little bemused.

"You see, Grace, greatness lies not in your achievements but in how you achieve them. There was once a great writer — I have forgotten his name — who wrote these wise words: *Conquest produces hate, hatred flames into revenge, and revenge results in destruction. And so the conquered become the rebels, and the rebels become the new conquerors, and the whole circle is completed, from the point at which it started.* In the meantime, millions of lives have been lost, and nothing has been gained. A union of nations cannot be cemented with the blood of slaughtered men."

"Why do we have wars, Mum? So many people killed, including Dad's parents."

"Not his parents, dear. His adoptive parents. Your dad was adopted by Mr and Mrs Brown when he was just three months old. Who his real parents were, we will never know…"

"Why did the Germans kill his adoptive parents?"

"Because they were Jews. I never knew them, but your father told me what wonderful people they were, and how much they loved him. Your father still misses them though it is fifteen years since they died."

"Where was Dad when the Germans took them away?"

"In France. The whole family had gone to Paris to visit some friends who had a twelve-year-old son exactly the same age as your father. When it was time for their return, they decided to let your father stay for another month to improve his French, and that, no doubt, saved his life. For not more than two weeks after their return, they were arrested and their house and possessions confiscated. That all happened in 1939, at the beginning of the war."

"What happened to Dad then?"

"Your father stayed on with the kind family in Paris, until he was seventeen. Then he left and joined the French underground resistance, that operated from a small studio near Montmartre."

"Does Dad still see them?"

"No. They were all killed in a bombing raid. It is all so sad, it doesn't bear thinking about."

"I would have liked to have a granny and granddad."

"Yes, dear, but we are lucky to have each other, you know."

"I do know, Mum. Do you miss your parents?"

"Yes, very often. I was only eleven when they both died in a car crash, but I have so many wonderful memories from the years that we were together. My mother liked to cook, as I do. I'm sure I inherited my gift of cooking from her. Every time I smell a new-baked cake, I can almost see her in front of me." Anna wiped her eyes with the corner of her apron.

"Oh, Mum! I am sorry; I shouldn't have made you talk about them. Don't cry, Mum."

Anna continued to cry softly as Grace hugged her. "Oh! I do miss them so terribly." She sniffed. "I don't think I will ever get over it. But how did we get on to this conversation?" Anna looked at Grace with red-rimmed eyes.

"Because I wanted to know why we have wars."

"Grace. Who can truly say why they happen? Perhaps it is because of a nation's greed, to gain power over that which belongs to others. And if you have a madman like Hitler, the instigator of the last war… who, with his powerful promises of a better world, a purer race, was believed by a group of fanatics, even though everyone else realized how unrealistic, even crazy they were… then everything gets out of hand. Millions of people killed in the most atrocious way. Cities and national treasures destroyed. They can be rebuilt and replaced, but the worst thing is that the spirits and souls of the survivors will stay damaged forever."

"Perhaps they will be taken into the Old Father of Wisdom's class, where he will help to mend them."

"The Old Father of Wisdom's class? What are you talking about, Grace?"

"You know, Mum! Before we are born. The Old Father of Wisdom, helps the damaged souls to mend again."

"Grace, dear, you are speaking nonsense. I think you must have been dreaming. There is no such person."

"There is, Mum. I met him before I was born. He has a long white beard, and fire comes from his mouth when he speaks."

"All right, all right, Grace. Let's say I believe you but I still maintain you must have dreamt it, you silly goose. Just let us hope and pray that the world will never see another one such as Hitler again."

"I am glad we didn't know him, Mum."

"So am I, dear. Evil men such as he, destroy everything which is beautiful and good in life."

"Why are some people so bad? I don't mean bad like Frederic, but really, really bad. Are they born that way?"

"I like to think that all children are born good, but sometimes something happens to them, either in their minds or souls, or both. Something they are not able to control. And that can make them bad. I don't know what the case was with Hitler or the Führer, as he was called. There are so many stories going around about his unhappy childhood, when his father beat him and his mother, missed opportunities and a misspent youth. It's hard to know what to believe. But one thing we do know is that in all the known history of mankind, rarely has there been one as evil and misguided as he was."

"Did Hitler have any children?"

"Not that we know of. He did marry his long-time girlfriend just before they both died, but I have never heard about any child he might have had."

"That is good, Mum. If I were his child, I would not like him as my father. But if he were, I would try to make him good again."

"God forbid, child… don't ever say such a thing. It makes me cold all over."

"Mr Smith, the butcher's son, Peter, was killed in the war. Do you think we should show him Dad's poem?"

"No, dear. It will only make him sad to remember."

"Will Dad ever make any money from his poems, Mum? Does anyone ever want to buy them, or will we always be poor?"

"Your dad is a great poet, Grace, but far too advanced for his time. People do not understand his style, and think it is too abstract. It is breaking his heart, but one day they will wake up to the beauty of his work.

Before you were born, we lived on a small farmstead just outside Guildford in Surrey. Your father grew a few vegetables and some fruit, and with our six hens and two cows, Daisy and Molly, we were able to feed ourselves."

"I remember, I remember!" Grace hopped up and down with excitement. "You stood in the doorway rubbing your big tummy, and Dad was chopping wood. I saw you before I was born. The Angel of Life held me up to look through a window so I could see who were going to be my parents."

"Oh, Grace! Grace! You do let your imagination run away with you, you silly thing. But…" Anna looked at her beautiful daughter with a frown on her face. "You are right; how you know, I can't say, but that is what happened on the day you were born. I stood calling your dad to get himself ready to take me to the hospital."

"Oh, I couldn't hear what you were saying, but Dad looked at me, and when our eyes met, I felt a wonderful warmth going through me, like I do when you cuddle and kiss me."

"That is called love, darling. And both your dad and I loved you from the moment you were conceived."

"Conceived? Do you mean when I was in your tummy?"

"Yes, dear. That's what I mean. But now let us go back to what I started to say, before you interrupted me. I also saw how it slowly destroyed your father not to have the time to write, as he longed to do. So, after you were two years old, we sold the farmstead and moved here to Ham, close to Richmond upon Thames, where your father hoped to get a post as a journalist on the local paper. But there were no jobs available and no money for us to live on, until I started to do home baking for the local baker. That provided us with just enough so that your father could carry on with his writing, and hopefully, soon, people will begin to understand him. It is all in God's hands, as they say."

"If God is so clever, Mum, why does he make Dad write something people don't want?" Grace looked at her mother, who was turning the dress over on the clothes rack.

"Child, we are never to question God's ways, but to trust in his wisdom, and all will be well."

The door opened into the room.

"So this is where you are... I thought I heard someone talking about me." Grace's father laughed good-humouredly as he unbuttoned his grey cardigan. "Phew, it's hot in here. Why have you got the heater on?"

Grace's father was an imposing figure, in his mid-thirties, heavily built with strong features. His sparkling sapphire eyes were fringed with thick black lashes that made him look almost feminine, that was, until one looked at his broad shoulders and his height of six foot four.

Harry Brown was very much the man of the house. Anna, her mother, was as petite as he was tall. She was only five feet two and in spite of her twenty-eight years, still had a childlike, delicate face and body. With her auburn hair tied into a ponytail, she looked like Grace's sister.

Anna Brown quickly told her husband what had gone on between the children.

"That little monster! I've a good mind to go and see his father; that pompous ass, if it weren't for his money, he would never have been made mayor."

Grace giggled to hear her father use her own expressions.

"Harry! Don't." Anna shook her head. "Grace has to learn to stand up for herself…"

"I know." Harry Brown stood pulling on the doorknob, about to go downstairs. "But at times I do feel so helpless and wish that I was a better support for both of my lovely ladies." He came back into the room and took each of them into his arms.

"But at the next town meeting I shall make sure I get him alone, and then I will give him a piece of my mind."

"Please, Dad," Grace begged, "don't give him a piece of your mind yet, you need it for your writing. Wait until you are rich and famous, then we will really show them."

"That might be years, my love." He tried to suppress his laughter as he stroked her hair. "Years, love," he repeated, "for it takes time for people to grasp the meaning of that which is outside their comprehension."

"Well, why don't you write something which is within their comp... re... mention?" Grace struggled with the pronunciation.

"When you are older, you will understand that each one of us can only be what we are. What good would it be if the plum tree started to sprout gooseberries?"

Grace laughed. "That would be very funny and make the tree famous, for everyone would want to see it."

"I can't win with you. You are just too clever, little lady." He gave her a hug.

"Be brave, my love." Anna kissed her husband's stubble cheek. "I—" she reached for Grace's hand, and looked at her with a beautiful smile. "—We, your two ladies, are doing very well. We both love you, and want you to go back to your work." She pushed him out of the door and firmly closed it.

"Come, Grace, you might as well change your underwear, too. Let's put a clean set on." Her mum helped her to undress and then put the garments into the soapy water in the sink. "Here." She opened a chest of drawers, and gave Grace clean underwear and socks. "Put them on quickly so you don't get cold. The air is still chilly in here, in spite of what your father said. That heater is not powerful enough to warm this room."

Suddenly the door flew open. Harry stood in the doorway, smiling broadly and holding a letter in his hand.

"I can't believe it! I can't believe it!" he shouted, looking pale and shaking. "Guess what this is?" He held a blue envelope so tightly, it looked like it was about to tear open. He waved it in front of him.

"This is a letter from the Poetry Society in London. They need a secretary and are asking me if I am interested in the position. And furthermore," he shouted, "they want to publish my latest poems in next month's issue of the *Poetry News*. They are paying me a hundred pounds in advance and will pay another hundred when they are published."

Harry Brown danced his two ladies around the room, one in her underwear, the other with wet, soapy hands.

"We will buy a new dress for you, Grace, so your mother doesn't have to wash every night, and with matching hair ribbons of your choice. And for you—" he looked with love at his wife. "No more baking bread long into the night. I will start taking over the household expenses, and *you*, my dear." He slapped her backside. "Can sit on *that* all day, doing nothing but growing fat!"

"Oh, darling, this is wonderful news for you. Finally, after so many years." Tears welled up in her eyes as she hugged him. "Oh, my dear, how truly happy I am for you. Nobody deserves it more than you."

Anna pulled herself together again. "The baking I will not give up. I like it. But perhaps I will confine it to this house, and I shall start right away by going into the kitchen to bake a celebration cake." She hung the underwear up to dry, then rinsed the sink. "Come, Grace, let us go to the kitchen, and bake the cake."

She took her husband's hand, squeezing it, as she whispered, "You and I will celebrate later tonight." She gave him a quick kiss.

"Mm, I look forward to that. Oh, and guess what else I sold today?"

They both looked at him.

"Ten pink toes." Harry laughed. "Oh! Oh! Oh!
Curiously came feet first
into this world.
Wriggling away
As if to say
Hello, Mum and Dad, we are here to stay.

"But wait,
There is more to see,
Two tiny hands,
A belly round and sweet
And then finally
The beautiful head of our darling Grace."

They all three shouted in unison and danced about, laughing.

Chapter 4

As the sun began to set, colouring the sky a glorious orange-red, Grace looked up from her plate of half-eaten chocolate cake and said, her voice full of wonder, "Look at the sky, Mum, isn't it beautiful?" She took another mouthful of cake. "Is it really true you can predict tomorrow's weather from the colour of the sky?" Fragments of cake fell out of her mouth as she spoke.

"Grace, for goodness' sake, don't speak with your mouth full. Here." Anna gave her a napkin. "Finish eating before you speak, and wipe your mouth. You look disgusting, covered in chocolate cake like that."

Grace swallowed quickly and then wiped her mouth. "But is it true, Mum?"

"Yes, dear, as far as we know today. Perhaps in years to come, we might be proven wrong, but as it is now, a red sky at night suggests a clear sky for hundreds of miles beyond the western horizon, and no imminent frontal system bringing water."

"Goody, goody!" Grace jumped off her chair then picked the last cake crumbs off the plate with her fingers. "I can't wait. Daddy promised to finish building the treehouse on the next sunny day. It is nearly finished; he laid the platform last week before the rain came down. You have to climb up a rope ladder, Mum. You will come and visit, won't you? It's not difficult to climb up, you just have to hang on tight, and don't look down if you are afraid. But I'll help you to get up there."

"With pleasure, dear lady." Anna laughed as she curtsied. "Will you send out a formal invitation, or do I just knock on the tree trunk when I arrive?"

Grace laughed. "Oh, Mum, you are funny."

Anna started to clear the table, then stopped and looked at Grace.

"Look, dear, in spite of the fine weather expected tomorrow, I think you will have to give your father a little time before you trouble him about your treehouse. He has a lot of things to prepare for his new position at the Poetry Society, before he starts next week."

"Clever Dad. Now people will understand him."

"Some, yes. Not all; everything takes time."

Grace drank the glass of milk her mother handed her. "Thanks, Mum. I love milk. Can I have another glass, please?"

"You certainly may. Drink as much as you like, it will help your new teeth grow strong and healthy."

"Why do they grow strong from drinking milk, Mum?" Grace put her fingers into the toothless gap in her mouth, where she could just about feel the edge of a new tooth. "Granny France told me the same, but when I asked her why, she just patted my head and said, 'Don't worry your head about why, ma petite, they just do'."

Anna poured her a second glass of milk before answering. "I expect Granny France thought you were a bit young to understand, but I will try to explain it to you, if you like." Anna sat down and poured herself a cup of tea from an old chipped teapot, added sugar and milk, then blew on it before carefully taking a sip. "Ah! That's better. Now, if you sit down again, I will tell you."

Grace sat down to hear the answer to her question.

"Within the milk there is a very small amount of something called phosphorus and lime," Anna began. "That is what makes your bones grow strong and your teeth strong and white. Within your jaw you have tiny, dormant germs, and when the time is right, they wake up and set to work in their cells. And with the help of some phosphorous and lime, begin to make themselves a kind of white armour, as hard as a stone, which grows harder from day to day."

Grace listened intently.

"You know what lime is?" her mother asked. "That is the sort of white pulp that you have seen standing in large troughs near half-built houses, and which the mason uses in making mortar. That is what the masons in your jaw use to build the teeth inside your mouth.

"As to phosphorus, I am afraid you will never see any, but you might hear of it. It used to be sold in the pharmacy in the form of white sticks about as thick as your finger. They have a nasty garlicky smell and are kept in jars of water, because they are very flammable.

They also have another interesting quality, whenever it is rubbed on a door or wall in the dark; it leaves a sort of luminous trail of a very peculiar appearance, which is called phosphorescence, from the name of the substance producing it. Phosphorus is also a very poisonous substance. People used to poison rats, with breadcrumb balls, in which it had been injected."

"Oh, Mum, and that poison makes part of my teeth?"

"Exactly so, and it even forms part of all your bones, and of the bones of all animals. The best proof of which is that the phosphorus of what are called Lucifer matches has been procured out of bones from the slaughterhouse."

Grace frowned, finding her mother's explanation difficult to understand.

"I can see that you are puzzled and ask yourself how these little teeth makers in the gums got hold of this terrible phosphorus, which is set on fire by a mere nothing, and which we dare not to put into our mouths? Where did they find the lime, which I also protest is not fit to eat and yet we have stores from top to toe? It is also very surprising to think of it being forthcoming in the jaw, just at the time it is needed there.

"Now listen, for we come to the important part. One day, when the blood was making its round of the body, it came across those little germs I spoke of, awake and eager for work. The blood knew at once that phosphorus and lime were what they needed, and together with a few other things which I won't go into now, produced exactly the right amount to begin the growing process.

"Now then, where did the blood obtain the phosphorus and lime? From that." Anna pointed to the empty glass on the table. "And in the milk you drank as a baby, there were both phosphorus and lime, though in very small quantities. There were many other things besides, in fact, everything the blood required for the use of its little workers within your jaws, to build your beautiful white teeth."

Grace looked slightly confused.

"Does that make sense to you, darling?"

"I think so, but it is very strange we seem to be made of poison."

"That is true, but there are also many other wonderful things, which we will speak about another day."

"I think I shall have a good look at my next tooth that falls out." Grace suddenly laughed. "Perhaps I will crush it to see if it strikes fire."

"You silly sausage; I think you had better leave it to the tooth fairy to take away. But what you must always remember is that by the law of nature, all things, with the exception of one or two, are good for us in very small quantities. But in larger ones, they will act on the body as a poison… and that goes for that cake, too, little lady. So leave it alone. Your stomach has had enough of that for today."

"Mummy, if Granny France asks you about the teeth, you'd better tell her, for I don't think I will be able to remember it all."

"I will, and I am so glad you think of her as your granny. She is such a lovely old lady and helped your father a lot during the war. Did he ever tell you about the day she hid Daddy under the floorboards of her kitchen?"

Grace's eyes widened. "No! How did she do that?"

"Granny France, as you call her, had a small cellar beneath the floorboards in her kitchen. She used it for storing wine and cheese. One day, on her way back from getting a few supplies, she suddenly heard shooting and shouting from around the corner, where two German soldiers were chasing a young, injured man with blood running down his face. As soon as he had passed her, she gave a loud scream and pretended to faint.

"As she collapsed, some over-ripe bananas spilled out of her bag and onto the ground. One of the Germans slipped on them and went flying. His gun ended up in the gutter and as the other soldier went to pick it up, a huge rat flew at him and bit him on the hand. With all that going on, the injured man got away and the two soldiers gave up the chase.

"Granny France collected the best of her spilled bananas and then walked back home as quickly as she could. She locked all the doors and windows and unpacked her shopping. She had just finished when she heard a slight tapping on the window. When she peeped out, she saw the injured man standing in a state of near collapse, holding on to the wall.

"It was your father. Granny France let him in. His flesh wound was not serious and soon began to heal. But because the Germans were still looking for him, she hid him below her kitchen floor, where he spent nearly a month before it was safe for him to leave again."

"Did she feed him the rotten bananas?"

Anna smiled. "She might have done. I don't know. But I did hear that Granny France got them from an old barge on the river where they had been left behind from some shipment or another, and was going to use them to bake a banana pie. I don't know whether she did or not, but that is something you can ask her about, when she next visits us. How long is it since she was here last? Was it when you were seven?"

"Yes. I remember because she brought me a lot of French books, telling me, it is never too soon to learn to parler Français."

"And have you practised?"

"No, but I like the pictures."

"Well, perhaps that is another thing we can concentrate on, if you have another day like today." Anna rumpled her hair. "You must always try to learn as much as you can, then you won't go far wrong."

Anna cleared the table, and then went to put the dirty dishes in the sink. "How about giving me a hand drying the plates?" she asked. "But please don't ask about the temperature of the water and how it is measured, for my head is getting tired after this eventful day, and needs to rest now."

"Sorry, Mummy, but there are so many things I want to know."

"I understand, love. Life is full of strange and wonderful things for us to discover."

"Will I have enough time to learn it all?" Grace nearly dropped the plate she was trying to dry.

Anna took it from her. "Concentrate on what you are doing, dear; you don't want to break the plates, do you? And don't worry your head about not having enough time. Everything you learn is taught by degrees, not all at once, and as you are a clever girl, you should have no problems."

"I am glad, because when I grow up *this* tall…" Grace stretched her arm up as high as she could, "I want to be a teacher and teach everything I know to the whole world."

Her petite mother laughed. "Taller than me! Then we will have to feed you on something else other than cake." She slapped Grace's hand as she was about to pick at the cake again. "How about a carrot salad?"

"With nails?" Grace licked her fingers. "I don't want any, Mum. I want to paint a painting for my new treehouse. Farmer Jones gave me a box of his daughter's old paints last week, when I helped to carry his shopping for him on my way back from school."

"Yes, that was kind of you and also of him. Miss Grey told me all about it. I do so appreciate her bringing you back from school every day; we are so lucky that your teacher lives just three houses away. But remember, Grace, however kind Mr Jones is, you must never, ever go to his, or anyone else's house, alone." Anna stretched to arrange the plates on the kitchen dresser. "Did he say how his daughter was getting on with her paintings in London? The last time he came over, he told me she was having an exhibition in the Mall."

"He didn't say, but he looked sad when he gave me the paints. Do you think you forget your parents when you grow up?"

"Sometimes, yes. There are children who want to cut the bond with their parents when they grow up, sometimes permanently, sometimes just for a period whilst they discover what is generally called finding their own two feet. But sometimes that can take years, and in the meantime, the parents suffer greatly from a feeling of being unloved. I hope Clare does change, for her dad must be feeling very lonely since Mrs Jones died last winter." Anna paused for a moment's thought. "Perhaps we should visit him more often? What do you say we give him the rest of this cake to cheer him up?"

"Mum! What about us? Then we won't have any."

"No, not of this one, little Madam Greedy, but I will bake another when the occasion arises. Mr Jones, I am sure, will never have tasted anything as good as this one before." Anna went to the cupboard and took out a roll of kitchen foil, carefully tearing off a piece and wrapping it around the remaining cake.

"I'll tell you what… since your father is busy at work in his shed, let's take it now, while it's fresh. It's not too late, it's only, let me see…" Anna looked at her wristwatch. "…six-thirty. Go and fetch your dress, love, it should be dry by now, and I'll switch the iron on. It won't take a minute to iron it."

Grace ran upstairs and quickly returned with her dress. "Here you are, Mum, it is completely dry. Stupid boy—" she mumbled the last remark under her breath.

"I heard that, Grace, and I told you to forget about it. I explained to you why Frederic is difficult at the moment, all right? Now don't let us spoil this beautiful moment. See how the sky is still coloured red? And later, when the moon and stars come out, we'll see if we can spot the Great Bear and the Milky Way up there."

Anna handed her the ironed dress, which Grace quickly pulled over her head. Then she went to the larder for a bottle of elderberry wine. "Let's be generous today, since it is a day of celebration." Anna packed the wine and cake into a wicker basket, before helping Grace into her coat and hat.

Farmer Jones, a stooping man of about fifty years old, but looking the best part of seventy, peered at them from beneath bushy eyebrows. He quickly buttoned his stained trousers.

"My dear, Mrs Brown. What have you there? And little Grace... do come in."

He moved from the doorway, and they followed him into a small and dark front room that smelt strongly of wet manure and was lit by a single naked light bulb that hung from the ceiling.

"Do sit down." He pushed some clothes aside from a grey, sagging settee that had a dirty blue blanket thrown over it. "I'll just go and put the kettle on for a cup of tea, and for you, Grace, a glass of homemade apple juice."

"No, thank you, Mr. Jones. If it's from your green apples I don't want any, it will be sour."

"Grace, that is very rude. I am sure it will be delicious," Anna whispered, then took her hat off and laid it next to her.

Mr Jones chuckled. "Little miss, there is such a thing as sugar, and if our dear God doesn't provide it for my apples, I will have to do it myself. Try it; I can assure you it is sweet enough."

Grace took a careful sip.

"Umm! You are right, it is delicious, Mr Jones." She looked up at him with a beaming face and took another sip. "Mummy baked a cake for you, only we ate half of it, for we are celebrating."

"Oh, why is that?" Farmer Jones put his cup down and stretched his legs. "They are getting stiff," he muttered as he started to rub them.

"Dad is going to London, to work as a secretary at the Poetry Society, and he is having his poems published. They are paying him a hundred pounds in advance and the rest when they appear in next month's issue." Grace spoke so quickly, she nearly choked on her drink.

"Good gracious, that is a lot to celebrate, but where will that leave you, my dear?" he asked Anna. "Will you then have to move to London?"

"Goodness me, I haven't even thought about that. Harry only heard the news this afternoon. But I suppose he will take the train from Richmond, to begin with, anyway. It's less than an hour each way. But we might have to move next year, when Grace will need a more comprehensive education, though I am delighted with her progress under Miss Grey's excellent tuition."

"Yes, she is a wonderful teacher, and very kind, too." Mr Jones poured a second cup of tea for Anna. "She was here yesterday to see if I had any news of Clare. Sadly, I haven't." He wiped his nose with the back of his hand. "Clare, as you know, was one of Miss Grey's students. She encouraged her with her painting and helped her to get a grant to study at the Slade School of Art, where she has won several prizes already."

"You must be very proud of her," Anna said kindly as she put her cup down. "I remember you saying that Clare is having an exhibition at the Mall; will you be going for the opening night?"

"I don't think so. Clare has no thoughts for me, only for her new friends and her paintings. Sadly, she has also got herself into bad company, where drinking and smoking pot seem to be the clever things to do. Frankly, I don't know what to do about it." His eyes filled with tears as he looked at Anna.

"Oh, my dear, I am so sorry." Anna touched his arm gently. "If there is anything Harry and I can do to help, please let us know. We will always be there for you."

"You have a kind heart, Mrs Brown, and I thank you."

He gave a loud sniff. "Since Martha died, it has not been easy for me; the work here is hard." He pointed outside to where open fields stretched as far as the eye could see. "The land has to be worked, and the animals need looking after, but since the war, the young men are not interested in returning to the land, they look for easier jobs in one of the many factories sprouting up everywhere. I really don't know what will happen to it all. What about Mr Brown… did they keep him in for long?"

"At the beginning of the war, Harry was too young, Mr Jones, but as soon as he was seventeen, he joined up in France, where he was staying at the time. Due to his excellent French and German, he was transferred to a desk job within the ministry where he worked as a translator, but at the same time, he was also involved with the French underground resistance. But that is something he will not talk to me about."

"No, I suppose not."

"You know, of course, that he is of Jewish descent, which meant that he had to stay in hiding. His adoptive parents also had to, but to no avail; they were captured here in England and sent to Buchenwald concentration camp in Germany, where they both perished. Harry always blames himself for not being there to help them. He has only now begun to settle down and is working hard on his poems."

"I know, my dear, I have heard about it. It can't be easy to live with something like that. And your parents, Mrs Brown… are they still alive?"

"No. Sadly, they too have died. In a car accident near Brighton when I was eleven. I was brought up by my dear grandmother — my mother's mother, and the only close family I had. But she also died, just before Grace was born. Life is not easy, Mr Jones. I sometimes wonder why we are tried in this way?"

"I wonder too, believe me, but somehow we have to make things work, and will just have to trust and believe that we can."

"Trust is a strong word, isn't it?" Anna wiped her hands on the napkin Mr Jones handed her. "We say it, but don't really practise it." She took a sip of the tea, which tasted sweet and strong.

"How do you manage to get your sugar, Mr Jones? The grocer never has any when I want some."

He laughed. "That's easy. I have an arrangement with him. I supply him with apples for cider, and in exchange, he gives me as much sugar as I want."

"Apples? The green ones?" Grace looked up from where she had been sitting, drawing.

"Yes, the green ones. Excellent for cider making if you add enough sugar. Would you like some, Mrs Brown? They are also good for making pies."

"Thank you, I would love some, but you will have to give me some sugar, too, as I used the last of mine for the cake."

"And a mighty fine one at that, Mrs Brown."

Mr Jones stood up and went over to the cool larder, where the shelves were stacked with sugar bags. He opened the door. "Just look at this." He laughed in a faint, crackling voice.

Anna was amazed. "My goodness! How did you get so many bags?"

"Aha, I told the grocer I would make the cider for him, free of charge, if he delivered the sugar. So he did. The cider is fermenting in the outside barn, next to Molly and Daisy, your old cows, who still give me excellent milk."

"I am glad to hear that. There are times when I miss our old life on the farmstead." Anna sighed, then finished her tea. "This has been a lovely evening, Mr Jones, but we will have to get going. Harry will be waiting for his supper, and this young lady needs to get to bed, it is close on eight o'clock."

She took Grace's hand. "We will come again to let you know how the pie turned out."

"I look forward to that, my dear." He helped her on with her coat.

"Here, Mr Jones, I have written a poem for you to say thank you for having us." Grace handed her poem to him.

"My dear, how kind of you. How did you know I love poetry? Sometimes when I feel lonely, I sit down and pen a few poems myself, perhaps you will come another day, then I will show them to you."

"If Mummy lets me, I will. Then we can share our writing, just like Daddy is going to do at the Poetry Society."

They left Farmer Jones standing on his doorstep waving to them, as they struggled up Petersham Hill with two heavy bags of apples, and six pounds of sugar.

"I told you, Mum." Grace looked significantly at her mother. "His daughter is no good!"

"We must not be judgmental towards anyone, Grace. We don't know all the background, only what Mr Jones told us."

"Don't you think he tells the truth, Mum?"

"Yes, I do, but the truth as he sees it. Perhaps Clare sees it differently."

"So truth is not really the truth at all." She sounded surprised.

"Some truth is more truthful than others," Anna replied. "Like the truth of you and I struggling up this long hill with a heavy bag of apples and enough sugar to last us until next Christmas. And the truth that I am tired and want to be in front of the open fire with my two loves next to me. That is a true truth. But some truths are like the wind; it touches on us, but before we have time to grasp it, it is gone."

Anna rummaged through her bag for the house keys, and then handed them to Grace. "Be a dear, love, and run and open the door for me."

Grace took the keys from her. "Oh, I don't have to, Mum. See, Dad is standing looking out of the window."

"Dad! Dad! We are coming, and bringing you lots of green apples and bags and bags of sugar." She ran quickly towards the house.

Chapter 5

When Grace was finally tucked up in bed, Anna and Harry sat down to discuss the day's events.

"I hope," Harry prodded his pipe with the end of a match stick before filling and lighting it. "I will be able to carry out my duties at the Poetry Society satisfactorily. After all, I have no special training, apart from my knowledge of languages and a first degree in English. And my love of writing, of course. It is such a wonderful opportunity… just imagine being able to work with today's greatest writers, and to get to know them personally. Oh, Anna! I can't wait."

"I know, my love, and don't worry, you will be as great an asset to them as you are to us. But what do you think we should do? Do we move to London, or are you prepared to commute every day?"

"I think in the beginning, I should travel every day until we see how things go. Grace will be eight next month, and in a few years, she will need extra tuition, she is such a bright little thing. Perhaps then it will be a good time to move. What do you think?" He looked at Anna and immediately carried on talking. "I have heard that St. Paul's School for Girls in Hammersmith is of a very high standard. The only problems will be getting her a place and the cost. Perhaps if you start to look into that now, then we can begin to plan ahead?"

"Great idea!" Anna popped a chocolate into her mouth from an open box on the table. "Don't worry about it; I will make an appointment with the headmaster next week, and see what he recommends." She sighed. "I shall miss Ham, you know. It is such a beautiful place, being so close to the river and with its many open spaces. I feel almost as if we are way out in the country; though the cottage is tiny, it is so peaceful with the open fields beyond the green."

"I shall miss it, too." Harry examined his pipe, which had gone out. "But everything changes, and we must change with it."

Anna put her arm around him. "You know, Harry, Grace has the most incredibly curious mind. Only today, I had to tell her all about the concept of her growing teeth. She appeared to understand and seemed to take everything in. I really can't imagine what she will do, when she grows up."

"Neither can I." He laughed. "Perhaps a dentist?" He struck a match and re-lit his pipe. "But we need not worry about that for a long time. I was thinking, as she is an only child, it might be a good idea to send her away to school when she is a little older."

"All in good time, Harry. In the meantime, let's just enjoy her growing up."

"You know, Anna, I am not altogether happy about Grace making friends with Mr Jones. I have heard rumours about him."

"Rumours? What do you mean? He seems such a lonely old chap."

"That may well be, but I heard someone at the pub the other night talking about his daughter, saying it was no wonder she left home, the way the old goat treated her."

"No, I can't believe it. He doesn't give me the feeling that he would mistreat anyone."

"One never knows what goes on behind closed doors, but I understood there was talk about him having sexually abused her throughout her childhood, and that was why she left and never wanted to see him again."

"Oh, Harry! Who would start such horrible rumours? I can't believe what you are saying... he always seems so pleased when we visit, and has never shown any sign of being that way when we are there."

"That might be so, Anna, but I would be happier if you found an excuse for not going there again. Don't frighten Grace about this, she is too young to understand. Just keep her away from him."

"Oh my God! You really have me worried now. If the rumours are true, then none of the little children here are safe."

"Exactly. That is why I want you to stay away from him."

"I will, but every time I meet him now, I won't be able to look at him. Supposing it isn't true? The gossip would destroy him."

"Grace tells me how Frederic and Jane are often over there visiting him, as Jane loves to see his animals. She is such a beautiful child, she always reminds me of the deer in Richmond Park, with her golden hair and big brown eyes. Miss Grey told me that she is extremely intelligent and one day will be a great intellectual. She is always top of her class."

"Frederic, the little monster." Anna laughed. "Just wants to play the piano. It seems that all his talents are in his fingertips. Perhaps he will be a great musician one day. He is going to Westminster next term, and the family will probably move to London soon, so Grace will miss Jane, and so will I; she is such a lovely child."

"Do you think Grace is lonely as an only child?"

"No, I don't." Anna shook her head. "I have never felt that. Grace has a very independent mind. She seems to be happy in her own company most of the time. She spends hours reading and making up stories which she writes down, then hides them in a box under her bed. I once asked her why she hid them there, and she said they need to mature before they are ready to be shown."

Harry laughed. "That's a new one; I like that."

"She is funny at times. I often see her sitting on that big rock over there." Anna pointed to a large rock about four feet by six, lying at the bottom of the garden. "Bathing in the golden moonlight. When I ask her what she is playing, she always replies, 'Not playing... thinking... remembering...'"

"Thinking about what?" Harry took a deep drag on his pipe.

"Just thinking, Mum,' is all she ever says." Anna shook her head. "Then at times she says, 'I must think, there is so much I have to remember'. So I just leave her sitting there, with her own thoughts."

"That's how it should be. All of us must develop according to the gifts we carry."

"I know, and you, my darling, are a wonderful husband and father, not forgetting a unique poet, which the whole world is about to discover."

Anna threw a cushion at him. "Just don't get too big-headed, for I like you the way you are."

"And I like you, Mrs Brown." Harry grabbed her, pulled her down on the settee, then started to kiss and caress her. "My beautiful wife," he murmured. "My little baker wife, I am going to eat you." He began nibbling her ears, then her neck, whilst Anna, giggling, tried to push him away.

"Oh no, my lovely little vixen, I am not letting you go, but perhaps I will start somewhere else?" He began to unbutton her blouse.

Chapter 6

Crisp autumn air drifting through the half-open window together with the shrill sound of the alarm clock, woke Anna from a deep sleep. She stirred Harry, giving up when he drowsily pushed her hand away.

"Another ten minutes, and I will come and kick you out, lazybones!" She pulled the blue-spotted duvet over his head before jumping out of bed.

"Where are my slippers?" She looked around and then spotted them in the far corner where she had slung them the night before. "I must get a new pair, these are falling to pieces." She looked with dismay at the side seams coming apart. Then the happy thought of going shopping and being able to buy what she liked took hold of her. In her mind, she was already spending Harry's first paycheque. The sound of the telephone ringing in the hall brought Anna back from her daydream. She quickly ran down the stairs.

Who on Earth can that be at this time in the morning? She thought, as she hurried to answer it, holding her dressing gown together.

"Anna? Hello! It's Jo." She sounded distraught.

"Jo? Hello there. What on Earth are you phoning so early for?" She glanced at the wall clock showing seven a.m.

"Have you seen the news yet?"

"News? No, I have only just got up. Why? What's happened?" Anna covered her mouth with her free hand as she yawned widely.

Jo, Anna's old school friend, who lived just a few miles away on Barnes Common, now sounded frantic. "They have found her!"

"Jo, what are you talking about? Found whom?"

"Jessica. The little girl from Kew who went missing last week."

"Oh no! My God... don't tell me she is dead?"

"Yes. She was found an hour ago, not more than a few hundred metres from my house."

"Dear God. Have they any clue to the murderer?"

"No, not yet. The police have just left after interviewing us. John and Susan, who are here on a visit, have gone over to the neighbours, to hear if they know anything else..."

"Oh my God, the poor, poor child."

"I know. Just five years old. Can you imagine the parents' grief?"

"Who found her?" Anna's voice was shaking.

"A woman who was out walking her Alsatian. The dog found her, half-buried under leaves and branches. She had been raped and strangled."

"Oh, my dear. No!" Anna sat down on the stairs shaking.

"I know the woman slightly, we have met occasionally. I will find out more from her when I see her next."

"Please do, Jo… and let me know what she says? Poor you, you must be feeling terribly afraid?"

"Petrified. Can you imagine having a pervert who is also a murderer, on your doorstep? I don't even dare to open a window."

"Do you want to come and stay here for a few days?"

"Thank you, Anna, but I will be all right. John and Susan were planning to stay for another week, but I am sure they will stay on for a bit longer now that this has happened."

"Jo, when they leave, do come and stay, at least until they find the killer. You know, I wonder if it is the same person responsible for the abduction of the other little girl who disappeared. When was it? Eleven months ago, near Wimbledon Common?"

"I don't know. Who can say? But it wouldn't surprise me. They never found her, did they?"

"No, not yet."

Harry opened the bedroom door. "Anna, when you are finished with your gossiping, do you think I could have some coffee?" he asked with good humour. He walked down the stairs, rubbing his eyes.

"Shush, Harry." Anna gripped his arm. "It's Jo," she hissed, "phoning about the little girl who went missing last week. They have just found her body, close to her home on Barnes Common."

"Oh, Christ! Anna, let me speak with her." He took the receiver. "Jo, hello dear. What a terrible thing to happen to you. Why don't you pack a few things and I will come over and collect you, in about half an hour."

"Thank you, Harry," Jo replied tearfully. "But as I said to Anna, I have my brother, John, and his wife, Susan, staying with me at the moment, so I will be all right, but..." Jo's voice was suddenly so loud, it sounded as if she was standing next to them. "If they don't find the murderer before they leave, I think I will take you up on the offer."

"Do that. You know you are welcome to stay as long as you want."

"I can't tell you how shaken I am. To think something like that can happen right on your doorstep." Jo was having difficulty controlling her voice. Harry, I must go now, the police are here again. I will phone you later." Harry put the receiver down with a bang.

"Goodbye, Jo, and remember, come as soon as you want."

"Christ almighty, that pervert! I hope they string him up by his balls when they get hold of him. And for God's sake, Anna, don't let Grace out of your sight, whatever you do."

"Don't worry, I won't." Anna looked towards Grace's bedroom. "But I had better get her up now. We are late for school already."

"If I wasn't starting work next week, I would take her myself." He put his arms around Anna, giving her a reassuring hug.

"I know, dear. But I trust Miss Grey, so don't worry about it." Anna suddenly had a worrying thought. "Harry, do you think it might be one of the inmates from the open prison on Ham Common?" She looked at him anxiously. "It has always concerned me with the prison being so close. All those prisoners allowed out during the day… somehow it doesn't seem right."

"It's impossible to say, but the police are pretty good at ferreting perverts out; usually they are well known to them."

"I suppose we will have to tell Grace when she wakes up, for she is bound to hear about it from the other children at school, but don't let's give her too many details," Anna said. "We don't want to frighten her. Come, let's go and make the coffee, I need a strong cup before we wake her up. Oh dear, I can't stop thinking about that poor little thing and her grieving parents. People who do that sort of thing should be locked up for good."

"If I had my way," mumbled Harry in disgust as they walked towards the kitchen, "I would castrate the bastard, before stringing him up."

Anna made the coffee and drank hers quickly, without adding her usual milk and sugar.

Harry finished his and turned to Anna. "Go upstairs and deal with Grace, Anna. I will make breakfast today. Call me if you need me."

Anna drank a second cup of coffee and then went slowly upstairs.

For the next few weeks, children were kept indoors. Rumours flew around, suspecting first one, then another. The open prison on Ham Common closed its doors to all inmates until further notice, as everyone in every household from Kingston to Putney was investigated, without success.

The police suspected it was the same person responsible for the abduction of the little girl in Wimbledon, and began looking for a serial killer, but again without success. The general feeling around the village was that whoever was responsible, let him be caught soon, so that life could get back to normal again.

The following spring, Harry finally finished the treehouse he was building for Grace. She and Jane decorated the old tree with pretty paper garlands, then asked Anna to bake a cake for the Sunday opening ceremony.

The girls grinned. "A huge cake... all our classmates are coming!"

Anna laughed. "I will look forward to seeing you fit all of them into that." She pointed to the pretty treehouse with its pink shutters and then went into the kitchen to bake a gingerbread house.

On the Sunday, at three o'clock, the children began arriving with their parents. They sang and shouted as they chased around the garden, climbed the tree and rolled on the grass, whilst their parents enjoyed a more sedate tea around the patio table where Harry had erected a large canopy as a shelter from the hot sun.

Anna found herself caught up in the festive atmosphere, and for a while, forgot about the fear and tensions of the last few months.

Harry decorated the children's orange drinks with cherry blossoms and then, pretending to be the Poet Laureate, placed a flower wreath on his head as he walked around the garden spouting Latin verses, to the amusement of everyone, except Grace, who cringed at his behaviour.

"Dad, don't act so silly, it's embarrassing." She held her hands in front of her eyes, begging. "Please, Dad!"

Susan and Brian Epstein told Anna about their success in getting Frederic into the music conservatoire in Marylebone Road, London, where he was to study the piano under Professor Gaetano, the famous Italian composer.

Then Grace shrieked, "Mum, there are some squirrels here! What shall we do?"

Anna laughed. "It is your party, dear, why don't you invite them to join you? After all, they are sharing their tree with you, so you can share your cake with them, though I suspect it won't do them much good."

"Okay." Grace then threw a large piece of cake down, and the squirrels quickly jumped down to get it.

It was late before the last guest finally left. Anna started to tidy up.

"What a perfect day and how lucky we were with the weather." Anna smiled as Harry lifted Grace up.

"Perfect." He grinned, looking at the half-dead flower wreath Anna was holding up and raising her eyebrows with a smile towards Heaven.

"I know." He gave her a hug and placed the wreath on her head. "I was playing the fool, but I enjoyed it. I will be back in a minute to help you clear up; just let me get this one into bed."

After that day, Jane and Grace fell into a pattern of spending more and more time together in the treehouse. Helga, Jane's au pair, would bring her over in the afternoon and then go off to see her young man, who worked at Crown's Garage behind the Ham parade. The two girls wrote each other stories and poems. Jane was especially clever at reciting anything classical.

Spring had arrived early this year, with pale green leaves appearing as blossoms unfolded themselves on naked branches. From the solid Earth, millions of flowers started to grow. The snowdrops gave way to hyacinths, daisies and forget-me-nots. Birds sang in the early morning, and in Farmer Jones's fields, sheep and cows were heavy with young ones.

New life began everywhere. Anticipation of warm summer days gladdened the hearts as old bicycles were taken out of the sheds and tired looking tyres pumped up, ready for rides with heavy picnic baskets.

Chapter 7

After six months at the Poetry Society, Harry was in his element, coming back each day full of enthusiasm and excitement, talking about such and such a poet he had been dealing with.

Anna, after a brief period of giving up baking, had gone back to supplying specially commissioned cakes to the Ham Parade Bakery.

Children were seen playing in the streets again, as life slowly resumed its old routine.

Jane and Grace were always together in spite of Frederic, who still tried for some reason to break up their friendship.

"If you don't want us to play together, go jump in the lake!" Grace shouted at him as she and Jane climbed up to her treehouse. "Oh no you don't..." She quickly pulled the rope ladder up as Frederic tried to get hold of it. "Get lost, will you!"

"Grace, why are you speaking like that?" Anna shouted out of the window. "Why can't you all play together?"

"We don't want him here, this is my house. He can go and play with his own friends," Grace shouted back.

"No, I can't," he said sulkily. "I have promised to stay with Jane." Frederic sat down under the tree, took out a book from his pocket, and began reading.

Anna shut the window and marched down into the garden.

"I don't like your tone of voice, young lady," she called to Grace. "You come down, this minute. If you are not able to behave yourself properly, then you won't have any friends coming here at all. Helga has brought both Frederic and Jane, and until she returns in an hour's time, you will behave yourself properly towards him. I will have no more of your nonsense."

"But he's a boy, Mum; we don't want to play with boys."

"That is still no reason for your behaviour. Frederic, come with me." Anna looked at him with a smile. "Let's go into the kitchen, I will make you a cup of hot chocolate, and those two madams up there." She pointed to the girls who were lying on their stomachs on the platform looking down. "Can stay where they are. And since they have pulled up the rope ladder, there is no way we can bring them any," she said in a raised voice.

"It is kind of you to take such good care of your sister," Anna said kindly as they entered the kitchen.

Frederic's jaw tightened. "I don't have a choice. My mother is completely neurotic towards her since the murder on Barnes Common." His piercing blue eyes narrowed. "If only they would find and lock up that bastard," he said bitterly, "but I don't see the point in discussing it."

"Perhaps not, but it doesn't change the fact that it has happened. Here, dear, I hope you like it." Anna handed him a steaming cup of chocolate and pushed a plate of biscuits towards him.

"How are you getting on with your music?" she said, changing the subject.

"Great, thank you, Mrs Brown. I love it, but find it hard with all the endless practising. All I want is to be left alone to compose my own music."

His eyes wandered to admire the dark wall panelling gracing the kitchen walls, then moving his hand, began writing invisible notes in the air as he sang 'In Hoc Signo Vinces.'

"I am afraid I don't understand Latin, dear. What does it mean?" Anna asked curiously.

"It means, 'In this sign you shall conquer'."

"I see."

Anna sat down opposite him. "I'm sure you will, too, if you keep practising. After all, you are only just thirteen years old; you have years ahead of you yet."

"I know, but nothing happens to my compositions. My masters just put them aside when I show them, then tell me in a patronizing voice to go and practise, as if I were a small child. I want to find a publishing company that will take me seriously... who are prepared to think, take risks, listen and be adventurous. Publishing compositions is an art, not a science." Frederic leaned forward, placing both forearms on the table, a posture that suggested confidence, even pride.

Suddenly, the door flew open. "Mum, Mum, come quickly! Someone is standing behind the hedge, spying on us."

"What are you saying, child?" Both Frederic and Anna jumped up and ran out of the door, down the garden towards the hedge and looked over it. There was no one to be seen. Frederic ran outside, looking down the road, but apart from an old white van just going around the corner, the road was empty.

Anna knelt down in front of Grace. "What did he look like?"

"I don't know, Mum, we just saw a bit of his head as he looked over the hedge. Three times he looked over, then ducked down quickly when we looked towards him."

"You must have seen something. What colour was his hair?"

"Just an ordinary colour, you know, like Miss Grey's and Farmer Jones's."

"You mean greyish?"

"Yes, but we didn't see a lot of it, just a glimpse."

Grace began whimpering with fright. "Do you think it was *him*, Mum, you know, the one who killed Jessica?"

"I don't know, but we are not taking any chances. We'll call the police and ask them to look out for any suspicious character in the area." She went to make the call, then turned to face them. "You two had better come inside until Helga returns." She pointed towards the kitchen. "I think there might be some chocolate left in the pot. If you have it now, it will still be warm."

Frederic came back huffing and puffing, having run all the way down both ends of the road.

"Are you sure you are not imagining this?" He looked at the girls with annoyance. "I didn't see anything."

"We *promise* he was there. Jane saw him first, and then a bit later, I did as well."

Anna came back into the kitchen. "The police are sending someone over to interview you. Now, don't be afraid, just tell them what you saw." She poured into mugs what was left of the steaming chocolate and went back to phone Harry.

Half an hour later, the police and Helga arrived at the same time. Anna quickly explained to Helga what had happened.

A young policewoman interviewed first Jane and then Grace, but neither of them was able to give any more information. Another police officer went out to look at the hedge where the two girls had seen him, and found several messy footprints, which were impossible to make out clearly. It looked as if whoever made them had deliberately tried to smear them.

"We have had some success in getting all the names of known child offenders in the area and are at present concentrating on them," the police officer said, as he went to the sink to wash his hands.

"You make it sound as if there are a lot, officer."

"There are, Mrs Brown. For instance, though I am not supposed to say this, there are at least fourteen of them living in one of the bigger council estates in Kingston upon Thames."

"I don't believe it!" Anna shook her head. "*Fourteen?*" she repeated.

"That's right. You see, when the offenders have served their time, well, they have to live somewhere. I mean, at least we know where to find them, but I have to agree it's shocking to send them back to a place swarming with children. If that's not asking for trouble, I don't know what is?" He shook his head sadly. "We must go now, Mrs Brown, but if anything else happens, please don't hesitate to phone again."

"Thank you, officer, I will." Anna saw them to the door with a troubled look on her face.

Two weeks later, when Anna had finished her work, she went into the garden. She inhaled deeply; the mild weather seemed to soften the sombre thoughts that had lain for months in her mind, like a dark blanket.

She bent down to pluck a few early crocuses, laughing as a rabbit shot between her legs and down its burrow. *Little monster... by tomorrow, all my carrot tops will be gone, but then I suppose we all have to live...*

Life could be so simple and perfect, she thought, and at that very moment, Anna felt so joyful, she started skipping, then twirled around, together with a few forgotten leaves blowing in the soft wind. "Where's Jane?" she called to Grace, who was singing away in her treehouse. "Is she not coming today?"

Grace stuck her head out of the window. "I don't know. She told me she had to do some extra work for her scholarship exam. She also wanted to stop by at Farmer Jones's to help feed the new lambs."

"I am surprised her mother let her go there alone."

"No, not alone, Helga is with her… except she always goes and sees her boyfriend when she is really supposed to stay with her. Jane told me she doesn't mind. But her mother mustn't know."

"I think someone should tell her that Jane is too young to be left alone."

"Why? Helga leaves her alone with us."

"That's different." Anna's expression was fraught with tension. "I do feel she is totally irresponsible, I think I will have a word with Mrs Epstein about it."

"Don't do that, Mum. Jane will think I have been telling on her."

"All right then… but I will have a word with Helga next time she comes here."

Satisfied with that, Grace went back to her singing.

"When you are finished with that song, can you come in and start your homework? I want to have it done before your dad gets home."

Anna bent down to pick some flowers for the house.

Chapter 8

"Hurry up, Jane." Helga, a robust blonde with high cheekbones set in a pretty German face, pulled Jane's arm. "Can't you walk any faster?"

"I can, but why do I have to? Farmer Jones is not expecting us before two o'clock. There's plenty of time." She smiled with anticipation. "The lambs are so cute. You must have a go at feeding them yourself, Helga."

"No way! I am not going near those little beasts. And anyway, I can't bear to think about what is going to happen to them in a few weeks' time."

"No, neither can I. I will never eat meat again. Never!" Jane stooped to pick a few daisies growing at the roadside. "I am going to make daisy chains to hang around their necks. Farmer Jones told me they like flowers."

Helga looked at her wristwatch. "Come on, Jane, if we get there earlier, then we will have time to go and get an ice cream down at Joe's Café."

"You always want to go there. I know why." She looked at her knowingly. "You want to see Peter at Crown's Garage. Are you his girlfriend?"

Helga blushed. "None of your business, young lady, but since you ask, yes, I do like him. A lot. He is going to teach me how to drive."

"Mama wouldn't like that."

"Why not? I can do what I like in my free time."

"Mama says it is not ladylike to drive; best to leave it to the men." Jane bent down to pick more daisies.

"Your mother needs to catch up with the times," Helga replied under her breath. Out loud, she said, "Jane, come on. Don't drag behind. The silly lambs are not going to care whether you give them flowers or not. All they want is their milk."

Ten minutes later they reached the farm, one of the very few left in Ham now, since they had opened the polo club and developed new housing estates around the river. Regarded as a little backwater, it was a short distance from the busy Ham shopping parade, with its quaint little shops and cafés, where Helga often went to meet Peter, who worked as a mechanic at Crown's Garage.

Jane ran straight over to the field where the sheep were grazing with their lambs.

Helga knocked on the farm door. Farmer Jones looked out of his bedroom window.

"Oh, you're here. You're a bit early." He grinned.

"I know. We have another appointment later on. Jane has to be back home before four o'clock."

"Well then, how about you come in for a drink with me while Jane looks at the sheep? We could have a glass of elderberry wine, and you can tell me what you think of it."

Farmer Jones closed the window and then came down to open the door. He looked as if he had not slept in weeks. His eyes were bloodshot and stubble showed on his face where he hadn't shaved for days.

"You are a pretty sight." He touched Helga's face with a dirty finger. "So soft with all that white and pink flesh," he murmured, taking hold of her arm.

I can't stand this man, Helga thought as she tried to ease herself away from him. *Something about him turns my stomach...*

"And what are you doing with yourself?" He leered at her, "When you are not looking after that little fawn." He pointed to Jane, who ran, laughing, after the lambs. "See your sweetheart, I bet?"

Helga ignored his insinuation. "I don't get a lot of time off, Mr Jones, but when I do, I am learning to drive. Peter at Crown's Garage is teaching me."

"Well, I'll be damned, now that's a fine thing to do. Sit down, my dear." He pointed to the settee.

"No, I'd better not, thank you. I have to look after Jane."

"She's all right. Look." He pointed out of the window to where Jane could be seen, stroking a small lamb. "She is so dainty. Nothing but a bit of tender lambskin herself…"

"Mr Jones, I had better be going out to her." She removed his hand from her arm.

"If I'd known you would be here so early, I would have shaved and changed my trousers, and then you might have wanted a drink with me. You must be feeling lonely, so far away from your family in Germany? I know what loneliness is. I have a daughter your age who left home to study in London."

"Yes, I know. Mrs Epstein told me how successful she has become as a painter. Do you paint too, Mr Jones?"

"No, I don't paint, but I do seem to have a small gift for penning words. Sit down, and I will show you." His breath was hot as he put his face close to hers.

"I can't, Mr Jones. I'd better go and see to Jane." She made for the door.

"Go then." He almost pushed her away. "I'll see to the milk for the wee lambs."

Aaargh! Helga rubbed her arm as if trying to rub away the feel of his hand. *What is it with that man? He gives me the creeps. Have a drink with him? He must be joking; I wouldn't go near him, the dirty old man!*

"Helga, come and see, isn't it cute?" Jane called to Helga, who was stroking a newly born lamb. "Look, it's sucking my finger."

Farmer Jones, who had come out with bottles of milk for the lambs, stood behind her, watching.

"Yes, look at that little beast, sucking away," he murmured with a shudder of passion. "It wants a teat in its mouth." His voice became thick, and a glob of spit dribbled down his chin.

"Here, my little one." He took hold of the lamb's head. "Open that pretty mouth of yours. Oh yes, that's right, you just suck away." He prized its mouth open. "Here, little one, open wide. That's it, oh, look at that little pink tongue! Here, take it all... oh yes. Oh yes, suck away, now."

He put the teat in its mouth. The lamb started to dribble the milk. "No, don't dribble it." He slowly wiped the milk away with a dirty finger, which he then pushed into its mouth. "There, that is good, isn't it? You know you want it, you little beast."

His voice was low with intense passion as he moved his finger rapidly in and out of the lamb's mouth, then suddenly gave a shudder as he looked at Jane, who sat innocently stroking the lamb's curly coat.

"Here, you hold it now." Farmer Jones handed her the milk bottle. "Get it to drink it all," he said briskly, before moving over to another lamb.

Helga, who had stood behind them, watching, looked at his turned back. *The dirty old pervert, I am not coming back here again. I know what he was doing, just look at the tell-tale marks down his trouser legs...*

"Jane, hurry up. Finish with that bottle of milk, and let's get going."

Jane took her jumper off and left it on the grass. "I will. Look, it has nearly drunk it all. But it is not late, why do we have to go so soon?"

"We just do. Now come on." Helga took the near-empty bottle from Jane's hand. "Just leave it here; don't bother to call Farmer Jones, he is busy over there."

"We'll have to tell him we are going," Jane looked at Helga's tense face, then stood up and brushed her dress. "Goodbye, Mr Jones," she called. "Thank you for letting us come." She waved as he turned around.

"It was a pleasure, little miss. Come again," he shouted back.

I bet it was... Helga looked towards him with disgust before taking Jane's hand and walking quickly away from the farm.

No more than ten minutes later they reached Joe's Café, at the Ham Parade. A privately owned café, Joe's was where local shoppers liked to sit and chat in its friendly atmosphere and restful décor of small round tables covered with red-and-white check cloths and modern prints on the walls. The café was packed with shoppers when Jane and Helga entered.

"What do you want to eat, Jane?" Helga asked as they sat down at a table near the window.

"Can I have a banana split and a cake?"

The waitress, a tall blonde woman with a cheerful smile, came to take their order.

"Hallo there," she said, looking at Jane, "it's a long time since I saw you last."

Jane smiled at her. "I have had a cold, but I am better now. Can I have a banana split and a cake, please?"

"Sure. And you, Helga?"

"I will have a cup of tea. Nothing to eat, thank you."

"Oh, I see." She laughed. "Peter is looking for you."

Helga blushed. "Oh... it's about my driving lesson next week. I will just run over and see him. Stay where you are, Jane. Don't move until I come back."

Helga quickly finished her tea, then grabbed her handbag and hurried through the swing doors, nearly colliding with a stout, grey-haired lady, carrying a black poodle.

"Can't you look where you are going, miss?" the woman grumbled. The dog barked at Helga as she tried to squeeze by, her short blue skirt swinging around her ample thighs.

Helga scowled at the woman and then waved to Peter. He stood in the garage doorway grinning, his nose and hands smeared with engine oil. Helga gave him a hug.

"I mustn't be long, *Liebe*. Jane is by herself in the café."

"What I have in mind, won't take long," he whispered in her ear, patting her pert behind and leaving a grease mark on her skirt as he led her inside.

The little café began to fill up as the weather suddenly changed. Black clouds filled the sky, and a sharp wind lashed raindrops against the window. The noise made Jane look up from the last bit of her banana split.

"Oh, no!" She looked with alarm at the increasing rain, then at the chair beside her. Swallowing the last mouthful of her food, she got up and ran out of the café.

About a quarter of an hour later, Helga came back to find the table near the window had been vacated.

"Jane?" Helga shouted, as she began wiping her wet face and hands with a paper napkin. "Where are you?" The other customer stared at her as she ran over to the door, which read Toilets. "Jane! Are you in there?" she shouted, pushing open the door marked Ladies.

Both cubicles were empty. *Mein Gott, where is she?* Helga began panicking and tore back to the table by the window.

"Please… has anyone seen the little girl who was sitting here?" With a shaking hand she pointed to the place where Grace had sat eating her banana split. She looked around at the bemused customers, who shook their heads.

"Helga, I saw her running out of the café ten minutes ago, when it started to rain." The waitress came over and looked at her anxiously. "I heard her shout, 'Oh no!' when the rain started, then she suddenly got up and ran out of the door before I had a chance to stop her. I thought she was running out to meet you."

"That's right, I saw her run outside." A young man, wearing gold-rimmed spectacles, who had been sitting reading *The Times*, got up from his table. "Is there anything I can do to help?" He looked with concern at the now weeping Helga. "Do you know where she might have gone?" he asked kindly.

Helga blew her nose. *She would not have gone home, or visited any of her friends without me...* She shook her head. "No, but thank you for offering to help. I will go with my friend, Peter, in his car, to see if we can find her." She struggled to control her voice. If not, I will have to go back... we only live about a mile from here, and tell her parents, before calling the police."

"Oh my God! Oh my God!" She began sobbing, holding her head in her hands. "What am I to do?" She ran out of the café, shouting across the road, "Peter? Peter? Come quickly! For God's sake, help me."

"Helga, whatever is the matter?" Peter came running towards her, wiping his hands on an oily rag.

Still sobbing, Helga tried to explain what had happened.

"Look, don't worry; you know what kids are like. She probably saw one of her friends passing by and walked back with them."

In the pouring rain? I don't think so, thought Helga, shaking her head.

"I'll get the car, and we will go and look for her. Just give me a minute to lock up the garage."

Helga sheltered in the doorway of the garage while Peter locked up and brought his car round.

"Hop in." Peter held the door open of his old Ford Fiesta.

Helga jumped in and slammed the door so hard that the car shook. "Steady on, girl. Don't take it out on this old lady, or she might fall to pieces," Peter reprimanded her.

"Oh, damn the car, just get going!" Helga shouted. "Drive down towards the river, then up the river lane towards Petersham Road and past Ham Polo Club. If we haven't found her by then, just take me back to the house."

The rain stopped as suddenly as it had begun and the warm spring sunshine rapidly dried the wet roads where only a few glittering puddles were left as a reminder of the storm.

Helga rolled down the window, straining her eyes as she tried to look in all directions at the same time. There was no sign of Jane.

"She couldn't have gone far." Peter's voice reached her, as if in a dream. None of it seemed real to her, it was less than an hour ago that they had sat in the little café together.

Oh, Jane, why did you leave, you stupid girl? I told you to stay put till I came back. Helga tried to come to terms with what had happened.

After half an hour of driving up and down the roads and finding no sign of her, they had no choice but to go back home.

Susan Epstein, Jane's mother, was gardening. Her head was covered with a large straw hat that had seen better days. On the ground stood an oval basket filled with a mixture of daffodils and tulips. She looked up, when she heard the car arriving, and then dropped the secateurs as Helga ran sobbing towards her.

"Mrs Epstein, I have lost Jane. I am so sorry... so sorry... I only left her for a few minutes."

"Helga, calm down, what are you saying? Where is Jane?" Mrs Epstein, a slim, glamorous blonde of thirty-eight, looked towards the car and suddenly understood Helga's gabbled words.

"Where is she?" she screamed. She took hold of the hysterical Helga and began to shake her. "Where is Jane? What have you done with her?"

"I don't know where she is, madam. Oh, I am so sorry—"

"Stop saying that, you silly girl, and tell me where you lost her."

"I left her eating her banana split in Joe's café, at the Ham Parade, whilst I just went across the road to Crown's Garage to see Peter about a driving lesson. He was busy with a client, so I had to wait for a minute." She blushed bright red as she went on fibbing. "It must have been about twenty minutes before I got back to the café, and by that time, Jane had gone."

"Gone where?" she yelled. "What do you mean, girl?" Susan started shaking her again. "Jane wouldn't leave just like that. Why did no one stop her?"

"The waitress thought she was running out to meet me," Helga sobbed. "It was raining heavily, she could not see clearly."

"Are you saying that Jane ran out in the heavy rain, and has now disappeared?"

Helga sobbed louder as she nodded her head.

"How could you leave her there alone? Don't you have any sense of responsibility, you stupid girl?" Susan slapped Helga's face hard.

"Mrs Epstein, don't..." Helga put a hand on her stinging cheek. "I said I am sorry—"

"Being sorry is not going to bring Jane back," Mrs Epstein shouted, running towards the house to phone the police and her husband.

Chapter 9

Ten minutes later, PC Thomson arrived. He was a stout, middle-aged man with a bristling moustache and an air of indefinable confidence and authority. Accompanying him was PC Littlewood, a tiny woman with brown alert eyes, a gentle smile and a concerned expression. PC Littlewood sat facing Susan Epstein and Helga, who went over the story once more.

"Can you think of anything that might have caused Jane to get up and run out of the café without a word?" she asked gently of the weeping Helga who sat nervously twisting her handkerchief.

"N-no," Helga stuttered in her anxiety. She felt physically sick.

"Mrs Epstein, when are you expecting your husband back?" PC Thomson started taking notes.

"He should be here in about half an hour." She looked at her Piaget watch. "I have sent my housekeeper down with the car to pick him up at Kingston Station," she replied, trying unsuccessfully to keep the fear out of her voice. She gave him a searching look as she picked up the telephone. "I can't believe what has happened," she gasped, as tears ran down her cheeks. "Excuse me a moment; I am just wondering if she has gone to a friend's house." She dialled a number and waited.

"Anna? Hallo, this is Susan, Jane's mother. I just wondered if Jane is with Grace?"

Susan frowned. "No, I don't think so, Susan, unless she has come in without me knowing. Just hang on a minute while I go and see."

"Grace?" Anna called through the open window. "Grace! Is Jane with you?"

"No, Mum, I told you she has gone to feed Farmer Jones's new lambs with Helga."

"Susan, she has not been here." Anna spoke rapidly into the mouthpiece. "Grace tells me that she and Helga have gone to feed Farmer Jones's new lambs. Is something the matter?" Anna asked, concerned.

"Jane has been missing for about an hour. The police are trying to find her... they'll be calling on you later."

"Oh my God, no! I'll send Harry over to help you look for her when he comes in. Oh, my dear, I am so sorry."

Susan put the phone down with a trembling hand. Her eyes were wild as she turned on Helga. "Something must have made her run out of the café!" Her voice shook. "Think, girl... did anything unusual happen at Farmer Jones's or on your way back from there?"

Helga shook her head, looking down at the carpet, as she shivered in her short and flimsy summer dress.

"Go and put a jumper on, you are freezing." She went to close the window.

Helga jumped up. "That's it!" she shouted. "Her jumper!"

"Now what are you talking about? What about her jumper?"

"She took it off when she was feeding the lambs. Oh, Mrs Epstein, she must have gone back to Mr Jones's farm to fetch it when it began raining."

"Right." Without hesitation, PC Thomson radioed to the station.

"Send a patrol car over to Jones's farm at Petersham immediately. We believe the missing girl might have gone back there to fetch her jumper." He listened for the reply. "Right, I'll meet you there in a few minutes."

"PC Littlewood, you are to stay here until further notice." He smiled briefly. "We will bring her back, Mrs Epstein." Then he tactfully turned his back as Susan broke down sobbing again.

PC Littlewood tried to calm her. "They will find her, my dear. Try not to worry, she might still be over at Farmer Jones's."

"She is so little," Susan sobbed. "Just seven years old, and now it's getting dark. Oh, Jane, darling, where are you?"

Brian Epstein, short, stout and immaculately dressed in a grey pinstripe business suit, burst through the door, slinging his raincoat and black bowler hat onto a chair in the hall.

"Is there any news?" he shouted to the police officer, ignoring his sobbing wife for the moment.

"Not yet, sir. Mr Jones appears to be out. The officers are waiting for a search warrant before they can go in."

"And how long will that take?" Brian went over and put his arms around his near-hysterical wife. "Shush, dear; take it easy, they will find her." He held her tight.

"No more than half an hour," PC Littlewood replied quietly.

"Half an hour! Anything can happen in half an hour." Brian banged his fists together. "Is there nothing else you can be doing?"

PC Littlewood could speak with authority when required to and did so now. "We are doing everything possible to find your daughter, Mr Epstein. We have patrol cars out searching the whole area, and a team of officers are already calling door to door at every house locally." She saw the despair in his eyes and softened her tone. "I'm sure we will soon have some news, sir."

Yes, but what kind of news? he thought.

"Oh Lord, for this to happen just now, when I am about to fly to America to clinch the deal for our new star campaign," he muttered.

Brian Epstein was the managing director of DBM, one of the most successful advertising agencies in London.

He raised his voice again. "Where is that bloody girl, Helga?"

"Leave her alone." Susan got up and poured herself a glass of whisky. "There is nothing more she can tell us."

"That might be true," he ranted, "but there is plenty I'd like to tell her before I send her packing."

Brian took the bottle from her and poured himself a large drink. "I don't suppose you drink on duty," he said to PC Littlewood, "but can we offer you some tea or coffee?"

The policewoman smiled. "Thank you, a coffee would be nice."

Her radio began bleeping. "Just a minute..." She pressed the receiving button. "Yes, sir, I understand. Yes, Mr Epstein is here."

"What is it?" Brian put his whisky down and tried to take the radio from her. "What have they found?"

"Mr Epstein, please... just a moment." She pushed his hand away. "Let me finish taking this call." She spoke into the radio again. "Yes, I will tell them." She ended the call.

"Well?"

"Nothing yet, sir. They are carrying out a search of Mr Jones's farm but so far, they have found nothing, apart from a small blue jumper lying in one of the fields. An officer is bringing it over for you to identify."

"Oh, that is Jane's!" Susan shrieked. "Oh my God! Where can she be?"

"Mr Jones and his white van are missing; my colleagues are out looking for him."

The shrill sound of a bell ringing made Brian jump up and run to the front door.

"Hallo, Harry. Thank you for coming." Brian spoke rapidly. "There is still no news, seems that Jones chap has done a moonlight flit. They found her jumper in his field."

"Jones? Do you mean Farmer Jones at Petersham Farm?"

"That's right. What is it, Harry? You've got a strange look, man. Is there something you are not telling me?"

"Well… I don't know if this is true," Harry said cautiously, "but there has been a lot of talk about him in the pubs."

"What do you mean — talk? What are they saying?"

"That he might have abused his daughter," Harry said awkwardly.

"Oh, hell! A pervert." He pointed to a tearful Helga who was coming down the stairs, still sobbing. "And that is where that bloody girl took my little baby. Why weren't we told about this?"

"It is only talk, Brian."

"Talk! That seems to be all everybody does around here. What we need is action, and I am going out myself to have a look around that farm. Come with me, Harry?"

Harry nodded. "Of course, anything that might help."

Brian opened the door to the lounge. "Harry and I are going to drive over to the farm to see if there is anything we can do."

Harry went over to give Susan a hug. "We'll bring her back to you, my dear." He nodded towards PC Littlewood. "Will it be all right for us to go over there?" he asked.

"Yes, as long as you don't get in the way of the search party."

"Get in the way?" Brian growled. "Why would we get in the bloody way? Come on, Harry, let's get going. Take a torch from there." He pointed to a corner cupboard. "And grab a bottle of rye as well, we might need it."

The farm had been screened off with police tape, and the scene was floodlit. Harry and Brian stopped their car some distance away then walked towards an officer on patrol, explaining who they were.

"We have nothing yet, but if your daughter is here, we will find her." He lifted the tape and let them through. "Be careful not to get in anyone's way," he warned, "and don't tamper with any clues you might find."

About twenty policemen were spread out over the fields, and the barn was lit up by searchlights, where a police team were examining every inch. In the house, a separate team was turning out cupboards and storerooms.

"So far we have found nothing here relating to your daughter, apart from her jumper," Sergeant Smith, the officer in charge, told Brian. "I can assure you we will do everything we can to find her, but we might have to wait until tomorrow to continue our search."

"And just what are we supposed to do in the meantime? If that bastard has got her, what do you think he is doing to her right at this moment?" Brian's anger rose. "And you are telling me to go home and wait till the morning!"

"I am sorry, sir. I know how you are feeling."

"No, you don't bloody know how I am feeling." Brian pushed past him. "You are only doing what is just another routine job to you, whilst my family and I are being torn to pieces."

"As I said, sir." The officer spoke with authority. "We will call off the search now and continue at first light tomorrow. In the meantime, a warrant for the arrest of Mr Jones has been issued, and special patrols are stopping and examining all white vans in the area. I suggest you go back and stay with your family and wait to hear from us. PC Littlewood will come back to your home first thing in the morning, and if anything happens before then, be assured that we will be over with the news."

"Come on, Brian." Harry took him by the shoulders. "There is nothing we can do here tonight.

Let's go back to Susan, she must be out of her mind with worry."

"No more than I am, man. What the hell am I supposed to do? Sit on my arse while some pervert out there is molesting my baby? I can't handle it." He aimed a hard kick at the stone wall, wincing as a sharp pain shot through his foot.

"Let me drive." Harry opened the passenger door of the dark blue BMW for Brian, who almost collapsed into the seat, trying to control his tears.

Chapter 10

Early the next morning, Chief Inspector Geoff White, in charge of the operation, called his team together. A tall, imposing man of forty-five, he had greying sideburns, a beak-like nose and a deep scar ran from his temple to his ear, distorting his otherwise clean features.

"Before we start, let me remind you that we are looking for a very small child... a little girl. She could be anywhere on that farm. Look in the rubbish bins, under floorboards, and turn the bloody barn inside out."

He gave a fresh-faced young officer a penetrating stare. "Officer Harris, you will be in charge of the team digging up the garden and surrounding fields. Seal the whole area off as far as the road and get someone to control the traffic."

"Yes, sir."

"And you, Peterson, will be in charge of turning the pigsty and stables upside down."

"Yes, sir." *Just my bloody luck,* he thought, *I will stink for days.*

"And Peterson?"

"Yes, sir?"

"Bring someone with you who can milk the cows. The noise from those poor beasts last night got on my nerves."

"Yes, sir."

"There is no need to remind any of you that this is the third child abduction we have had to deal with in a very short space of time." The inspector slammed his fist down on his desk. "I want results, and fast," he said in a steely voice.

There was a moment of earth-shattering silence, before he continued. "Now get going, all of you. It's ten to seven; I want you all over at the farm and hard at work no later than seven." He made a note in his folder before closing it. "That's it. I expect full reports from all of you before midday." He took a deep, audible breath.

A chorus of voices replied, "Yes, sir."

The team quickly filed out, and seconds later were running to the awaiting cars.

Inspector White pressed a button on his radio and spoke rapidly. "Operation 623 commencing at seven. Over and out." Then, as if carrying a heavy burden, he walked slowly out to his black Mercedes.

"Morning, sir," the driver touched his cap then opened the car door for him.

"Morning, Hans."

Inspector Geoff White looked ironically at the sky before getting in, for it seemed to him that the sun had never risen so brightly and with such sparkle, as on this morning.

"Take the track through the common, Hans."

"Yes, sir."

A dusty track led through Ham Common to the main road. The common itself was ringing with birdsong, and along the path, a small brown deer left its grazing to skitter away through the bushes as the car approached.

The inspector tried to disguise his feelings by assuming an expression of calm assurance. He leaned back, closing his eyes and seeing again the vivid mental image of little Jessica's mutilated body, discovered on Barnes Common only six months ago.

"Where do you want me to stop, sir?"

Hans's voice brought him out of his reverie. "Over there." He cleared his throat and pointed to a gap in the mass of police cars surrounding the sealed off farm.

It was just after midday. PC Peterson swore under his breath, as he heaved yet another shovel full of manure. "Bloody shit!" He threw it down, and then aimed an angry kick to another huge pile. "I've had it! Mabel's going to love me tonight, stinking like this." He wiped his sweaty forehead with his sleeve. *Let someone else do this for a while.* He stabbed the shovel into a mountain of rotting manure and began to walk away, when he suddenly spotted something sticking out near the bottom of the pile. It looked like the corner of a handkerchief.

He gave it a gentle pull, then went pale. "Oh my God! Sweet Christ Almighty... Chief! Chief!" His voice was shaking. "Over here!"

"Peterson?" Chief Inspector White came running. "What have you got?"

Peterson pointed to the pile, where a small skeletal hand, partly wrapped in a red cloth, could be seen.

"Stand aside, man... and someone get me a pair of wellingtons!" the inspector shouted over his shoulder, pushing Peterson away. "And get me a team over here, fast, to seal this cesspit off."

He took the shovel and carefully removed more of the manure from around the hand. "This is not the child we are looking for; it's clearly been here for some time."

Peterson took the shovel from the inspector who spoke into his radio. "Get the pathologist over here, quick as you can... yes, that's right... in the pig sty... what? No, no, not the missing Epstein girl, but... we are dealing with mass murder here." The inspector paused for a moment, his deep frown accentuating the scar on his temple.

"And John, get more patrols out as far as central London; I want this bastard brought in, and fast... no, by the state of it, the hand must have been here for at least six months, not a scrap of flesh on it... yes, in the pig sty... hm, that will be for the pathologist to say... oh, just now... right, I'll be back later with a full report."

The inspector clicked his radio off as a forensic team hurried over and began screening the area off.

Later the same day, they found Jane in Mr Jones's white van on Ham Common. She had been raped and strangled and then thrown under a filthy horse blanket in the back of the van like a lifeless rag doll.

"This is one sight I will never forget." The inspector spoke in a low, agitated tone to PC Harris. "That poor child's mutilated body, and so callously tossed aside… left to rot under a stinking blanket. The pervert must be mentally deranged." He rubbed his eyes and inhaled deeply before composing himself. He now had to face the unenviable task of breaking the news to the Epsteins.

A red-eyed Brian in his shirtsleeves answered the inspector's ring at the door.

"Mr Epstein, may we come in?"

Brian looked at their serious expressions. "Oh, God, no! Don't tell me… No! God, no!" His face crumpled and tears began streaming down his cheeks.

"I am so sorry, sir. May we go through? I'm afraid I have to ask you some questions."

"Brian? Who is it?" Susan came running down the stairs, her blue silk robe flowing behind her. She looked at her weeping husband, then at the police.

"You've found her! Where is she?" She looked around frantically, and then the realization suddenly struck her. "She's dead?" she whispered.

"I am so sorry, madam." PC Harris bent his head.

"Noooo! Not my baby... no! Jane, *Jane*!" She screamed helplessly, like a wounded animal, before collapsing in a heap at the bottom of the stairs.

Brian bent down to her, as Frederic came running in from the garden. "Frederic, call the doctor," he urged through his sobs.

Frederic ran through the doors into the lounge.

"And get Mary from the kitchen, tell her to bring some water!" Brian shouted after him.

Frederic was shaking as he put the phone down. "He'll be here in a few minutes, Dad." He looked at Inspector White, desperately trying to control his emotions. "It's my sister, isn't it? Is she...?"

"Come on, son." The inspector took him by his shoulders. "Let's go and sit down until the doctor arrives."

"Where... did they... find her?" Frederic's throat was so dry he could hardly get the words out.

"In Mr Jones's van, on Ham Common, no more than a mile away."

"That rotten stinking pervert! I am going to kill him. Where is he?"

"Now, take it easy, son. We haven't found him yet. But we will, and then he will get his just punishment."

"Just punishment, my foot!" Frederic shouted. "I've seen the 'just punishment' as you call it, which is dished out to the bastards living in luxury accommodation on Ham Common!"

Frederic threw himself onto the piano stool and began hammering his closed fists on the keys.

"For Christ's sake, stop that infernal noise, Frederic!" his father shouted through the open door. "Don't we have enough to deal with, without you destroying a ten-thousand-pound Steinbeck?"

Frederic slammed the piano lid down and then ran, sobbing, out of the room.

Susan came round just as the doctor arrived. Her screams tore into the air, and then she began retching and gasping for air.

"Let's carry her into the lounge." Doctor Davidson was the family's GP. Tall, slim and grey-haired, his tired blue eyes quickly assessed Susan's condition. "She's hyperventilating; put her on the settee and get some blankets."

Susan struggled and tried to speak and then felt the sharp sting of a hypodermic needle.

Chapter 11

"Harry, why don't you go up and speak to Grace? I can't bear listening to her crying. She hasn't stopped since she went to bed. I have tried to comfort her, but nothing helps." Anna gave her husband a look of helplessness. "I don't know what to do." She blew her nose.

Harry folded *The Times* and laid it on the coffee table before getting up.

"I'll go and sit with her, love." He looked pale and drawn. "Jane was her best friend, Anna; I don't know if she will ever get over her death. I know for certain I won't. Oh, Christ! I blame myself."

"Why?"

"For not telling Brian and Susan the rumours about that filthy pervert."

"Don't, Harry. You were not the only one who had heard the stories. Oh, do go up to Grace, love. I would go myself, but I have promised to give Susan a call, though I dread speaking to her... I mean, what can we say, apart from sorry?

"But I can't for the life of me understand why Jane would run back to the farm in the pouring rain just to get her jumper. Why not wait for Helga to come back?"

"The police spoke to the young man, Peter, at Crown's Garage. Apparently, he and Helga were not looking at available times for driving lessons, but engaged in more intimate matters. It was nearly half an hour before she was back at the café. When Helga was interviewed, she told police that the jumper was a gift from Jane's grandmother and she had been told to take extra special care of it. I suppose the child was worried the rain might ruin it." Harry sighed and gave Anna a hug. "When you're finished speaking with Susan, put the coffee on? My head is splitting."

Grace lay sobbing under her duvet. "Daddy, why did he do it? Why did he kill her? Why, Daddy?"

Harry listened to the muffled little voice. *Why indeed?* "Mr Jones is a very sick man, Grace, with uncontrollable urges that make him kill."

"But Daddy, he was our friend. We wrote poetry together."

"No, Grace, he was not a friend. He only pretended to be in order to gain your trust. In time, he would try to hurt you, too. None of us saw him for what he really was."

"Daddy, now I remember. He was disguised as an apple."

"Grace, dear, what are you talking about?"

"You know, Daddy… before I was born. On my way down to Earth, I met him; he disguised himself as an apple and then stole some of my letters. Now I understand why I liked what he wrote so much."

"Look, Grace, I think you need to sleep now and try not to let your imagination run away with you. But you are quite right! He was in disguise; none of us recognized him for what he really was."

"What will happen to him now, Dad?"

"He will be locked up for the rest of his life, perhaps in a mental institution. Grace, your mother and I are seriously thinking about moving away from here. Leave all the bad memories behind us. What do you say we move to London? You will make new friends there and go to a fine school. That will take your mind off things."

"Oh, yes, please, let's, Dad," she pleaded. "I don't want to live here any more without Jane. How did the police discover where she was? And why did she go back to the farm?"

"The police interviewed everyone in the area, including me."

"Why you, Dad? You would never do such a wicked thing—"

"No, of course I wouldn't, but the police didn't know that. Anyway, they interviewed everyone, including Mr Jones, and later on, when they searched his grounds, they found Jane's jumper, which she had taken off and left behind after feeding the lambs. Then they pieced the whole story together. When it began to rain, Jane remembered leaving her jumper and went to get it, and that was when Mr Jones got hold of her." Harry sat down on her bed and gave her a cuddle.

Grace then began telling him about the other characters she had met on her way down to Earth.

Harry went pale as he listened, then gently put his hand over her eyes. *Oh my God, how on earth did she get to make up those characters so realistically?* He looked at her strangely. "Go to sleep now, love. You can tell me more about them tomorrow." He kissed her brow, put the light out and left his daughter to rest.

Chapter 12

With tears in her eyes, Anna put the receiver down and went to stand in front of the open window.

"Where are you now, little girl?" she whispered, as the soft evening breeze caressed her face, and stars glittered in the clear sky. "Darling little girl, why did you have to die in this horrible way?" She looked questioningly at the waning moon. "Why? Why? Why? Where is the love and beauty we have been taught to believe in? If there is a God, answer me now, for I don't have the strength any longer to try to work it out."

An unbearable pain wrapped itself around Anna as she quietly closed the window. She went over to the kitchen table and sat down heavily on a white painted chair. She absentmindedly brushed up some crumbs from the table, looked at them, but not having the will required to get up and dispose of them, she let them drop back on the table.

It doesn't really matter what the house looks like, she thought, and looked at the crumbs as if they could hear her. *Nothing matters any more. Oh, little Jane, how we will miss you.*

"Anna, are you all right?" Harry came into the kitchen from the garden where he had been trying to clear his mind in the cool air.

She reached up for Harry's hand, as he leaned over from behind her. "I will never be the same again. I don't know what I am feeling any more, apart from this pain that is tearing me to pieces."

Harry stroked her hair. "Was it that bad, speaking to Susan?"

All Anna could do, was nod her head as the tears ran down her cheeks. "Worse," she whispered.

Harry poured himself a cup of coffee. "One for you, love?"

Anna shook her head, continuing to cry softly.

"Darling, we are going to have problems with Grace." Harry sat down. "I don't know what to make of her. She feels it is all her fault that Jane was killed."

"Her fault?" Anna looked at him, sniffing. She blew her nose.

"Yes. She keeps saying that she should have recognised that sick pervert—"

Anna looked up sharply.

"Sorry, she did say Mr Jones, dear; it's me that can't think of him as anything other than a sick pervert… anyway, she said she should have recognised him for what he was, in disguise."

"I don't understand, Harry. What disguise?"

"I don't understand, either." He finished his coffee, then went over to the sink, rinsed his cup and left it upside down to drain. Pulling out a chair, he sat down at the table facing Anna. He looked at her seriously.

"Just listen to this. Grace told me a strange story, about how she had met Jane, before they both were born."

Anna frowned as her husband continued.

"Jane was disguised as a fawn, as she was not strong enough to carry the intellect she had chosen to bring with her to Earth. She also met Mr Jones, who had disguised himself as an apple."

"Harry, please, I am not in the mood for this nonsense."

"Anna, it is serious, please listen."

"No, Harry!" She raised her voice.

"Shush, Anna! Grace will hear you."

Anna stood up, holding her hands over her ears. "Are you telling me she is having a nervous breakdown? Please! Not that, on top of everything else," she whimpered.

"Anna, I don't think it is anything like that. She is so convincing when she speaks."

"But where is she supposed to have met them before?"

"On the stairs."

"The stairs? What stairs?" She raised her eyebrows and wearily shook her head.

"The stairs on the way down to Earth. She told me in a calm voice that she should have realised that all the characters she had met on her journey to Earth would somehow be part of her life. I asked her who else she had met—"

"Harry, I am surprised at you. Why encourage her fantasies?"

"Frankly, I was curious." He looked worried. "Grace then told me about the others."

"What others?" Anna opened a tin of biscuits and passed it to him.

"No thanks, I'll have my pipe." He took the pipe from his pocket and lit it.

"Try one, Harry, they are from a new recipe. Tell me what you think."

Harry took a biscuit and bit into it. "Delicious. I like the combined flavour of ginger and honey. Are you going to sell them at the Baker's shop?"

"I am trying to, but so far Mr Stone is not convinced that his customers will like them."

Harry finished the biscuit. "Anna, I know you are trying to resume normality with this conversation, but we really must talk about Grace. I am concerned about what goes on in her mind. It's not the first time it has happened; do you remember when you told me how she had seen you and me before she was born? What was it she said? I remember… 'Mum, the Angel of Life held me up to a small window to show me my Earth family.' She then went on to accurately describe you and me and what we were doing at the time."

"Harry." Anna slipped into his outstretched arms. "We are all in deep shock. Perhaps this is her way of coming to terms with what has happened."

Harry shook his head, then inhaled deeply on his pipe before answering. "I am not so sure."

Anna stood away from him. "You worry me. What is it? What else did she say?"

Harry paled. "She told me that the first character she met was an evil person, who had a huge bag with the word Power written on it, and how the letters had run like a river of blood towards Earth. She then went on to tell me that the character had told her he was in a hurry, so that he could get down before her."

"And who, of all the people she knows, does she think he is?" Anna raised her voice.

Harry turned his back, pretending to re-light his pipe so that she should not see the pain that darkened his eyes.

"You frighten me." Anna took hold of him and turned him around to face her. "Tell me what she said!"

"The Führer." Harry said it quietly, almost as if to himself.

"The Führer? You mean…"

Harry nodded. "Yes, Hitler."

"But Hitler is dead. He died before she was born. How is he to be part of her life? Oh, of course!" She slapped her forehead softly with her hand. "Sorry, my love, if what she is saying is true, it must be to do with your adoptive parents dying at Buchenwald." She hugged him. "But Harry... Harry, this is crazy. Let's get a grip on ourselves and not get carried away by Grace's fantasies—"

"They are not fantasies, Mum!" Grace shouted from the top of the stairs where she stood in her long white nightdress. "It is all true. But no one ever believes me," she sobbed before running back to her room and slamming the door.

"Oh my God, she has heard everything." Anna ran up the stairs after her. "Grace, open the door this instant!" Anna rattled the doorknob. "Open up... now!"

"I won't, Mum, not before you say you believe me."

"Grace, just stop this nonsense. I have had enough. I will come back in five minutes, and you had better have the door open by then."

Anna walked slowly down again.

"Harry, we must be careful with her, otherwise, we might have to take her to a child psychologist." She broke off. "You are not saying anything. What is it?"

"Nothing." Harry took a pipe cleaner and attacked his pipe. "All this has really shocked me, that's all. I mean, imagine... that swine's a mass murderer, and how many times have you and Grace been over there, never suspecting anything? Incredible!

"The police are tearing his place to pieces. But so far, they've found nothing, apart from that poor little girl, Hannah, from Wimbledon, buried in the pigsty. And a stash of pornographic magazines and videos concealed in a space above the hayloft. The monster; he should be strung up!"

"And they haven't found him yet?"

"No. He seems to have disappeared into thin air." Harry stopped speaking and listened. "Anna, is that a car coming?"

"Yes, I can hear the wheels on the gravel." They both ran to the window and watched as Brian Epstein got out of his classic grey Daimler. Harry went to open the door, whilst Anna began clearing the coffee away.

"Brian! Hello, mate, come on in."

Harry stood aside as Brian, covered in mud and with blood running from a deep cut on his forehead, quickly shut the car door and ran into the house.

"My God, man! What's happened to you?"

"Get me a whisky, Harry," said Brian as he slumped down on a chair and buried his head in his hands.

Harry poured him a large scotch, leaving the bottle there, then sat down facing him. Anna ran to fetch some water and a towel.

"He's dead. They'll find him in the morning." Brian's voice could barely be heard over the sound of running water.

"Dead! Who is dead? Speak up, man." Harry gently shook Brian. "What are you talking about?"

"We found him." Brian gulped the drink then put the glass down. "He hanged himself. They'll find him in the morning."

Harry refilled Brian's glass. "Who hanged himself?"

"That filthy, rotten bastard, who killed my beautiful little baby." He bent his head over the kitchen table and started sobbing.

Anna and Harry stared at each other in horror.

"I think you should go up and see to Grace, Anna," Harry said.

"Yes." She put the water and the towel down on the table and went quietly out of the room.

"Brian? Now tell me what you have done!"

"Nothing more than any decent man would have done, and what that lousy pervert deserved. We strung him up! Tom, my brother-in-law, and I have been searching for that bastard for the last two weeks." His hand shook as he dabbed at the bleeding wound on his forehead. "The police are hopeless, for all their manpower. They don't come up with anything."

"So you took the law into your own hands?" Harry dared not believe his thoughts.

Brian emptied the glass with one swallow. "Yes, I did."

"After Jane's funeral last week… oh, my God, that poor little thing, I can't bear it." Brian started sobbing again. "I can't bear it, I tell you." He blew his nose loudly. "Anyway, I promised myself that I would not give up until I found him, even if it took me the rest of my life."

"But how did you know where to find him?"

"Somehow I knew he would not go far from his precious farm. Every night, Tom and I had been lying in wait for him on the common, close to that part that backs on to his fields. We took a length of rope with us, with the intention of tying him up, before handing him over to the police. Well, we finally spotted him tonight, creeping out from some sort of underground cave that must have been used at one time for storing potatoes and fruit.

"It's now completely overgrown and impossible to see from the outside. We followed him as he made his way to the farm, where he got hold of one of his cows and started milking it. The bloody swine, he looked half-starved.

"That was when we made our move and caught him. There was a fight. Even the cow kicked me." Brian pointed to the cut and dabbed it again. "When we finally managed to overpower him, we dragged him kicking and swearing down to the apple orchard and there… well, hatred got the better of me, and with Tom's help, I slung the rope over one of the branches and strung him up." Brian poured himself another large drink and gulped it down.

"For Christ's sake, Harry, don't look at me like that. We had to do it, can't you see? If the police had caught him, what would the courts have done? Got some psychiatrist to testify that the balance of his mind was disturbed and then lock him up in a nice cosy hospital for a few years, before letting him out again to carry on his filthy work where he left off?" Brian banged his closed fist on the table. "I was not going to let that happen."

"And where's Tom?"

"Tom's on his way to Amsterdam as we speak. He's catching the ten o'clock flight, and as it happens, I'm already booked on a flight there tomorrow, because I genuinely have some business appointments there. I'm glad, because I don't want to be around when they find him. I'd like to get on the eleven-thirty flight, Harry. Will you drive me to the airport? And keep the Daimler in your garage until I return in three days' time?"

Harry opened his mouth and shut it again, unsure what to say.

"If the police come here and ask you about my car, all you have to say is that I spent the evening with you and Anna and had too much drink, so you drove me to the airport. That much is true, at least." He held up the nearly empty whisky bottle.

"Oh, and another thing — I need a bath and some clean clothes to travel in." He brushed his jacket where the mud was drying. "My suit and passport are in the car. I phoned Susan when I left the office to tell her I was going to see you after work. She won't be expecting me back yet. I'll phone her on the way to the airport and give her a plausible story."

Harry listened, stunned. All he could do was nod his head. Then he pulled himself together.

"Brian, if you want to catch that plane, you'd better hurry up. It's ten o'clock now. I'll go and tell Anna and find you some clean clothes. Leave the bathroom door unlocked."

"Harry." Brian grabbed his friend's arm. "Don't tell Anna about this; let it be just between you and me?"

"That will be hard, Brian, but perhaps it's better that way, though I'm sure she will suspect once the news gets out."

"Thanks, mate." Brian got up and then stumbled, finding himself sitting in the chair again.

"Oh, God, wait a minute; let me help you." Harry took his arm and marched him slowly upstairs to the bathroom, found him some clothes and then went back to the kitchen to make some more coffee.

"Jesus bloody Christ," he murmured to himself, "what am I going to tell Anna?"

"Nothing." Anna joined him in the kitchen. "I was in the lounge and heard everything. God, what a mess! In a way, I don't blame him for what he has done, but I am terribly worried about you getting involved."

"I know, love. I'm sorry, but I have to help him; he would have done the same for me." He poured a cup of coffee, cooled it with milk from the fridge and drank it in one go. He hugged Anna. "Oh, my love, whatever happened to our beautiful, peaceful life? Hm?" He stroked her cheek. "Will our lives ever be the same again?"

Chapter 13

After that disastrous spring, Harry and Anna decided it was time for them to move to London and begin looking for suitable schools for Grace to attend.

"We talked about St. Paul's School for Girls in Hammersmith." Anna looked over her reading glasses at Harry, who sat studying the last *Poetry Review*.

"Yes, how did you get on with the headmaster when you phoned him last week?"

"Not very well, I'm afraid. Apparently, there is a waiting list of about five years. Most parents, he told me, put their child's name on the waiting list when they are born. It's the same with all the first-class schools."

"Ridiculous!"

"That may be, but we have a problem. Where on Earth do we send her?"

"I have an idea. Why don't we ask Mr Collins, my boss? He has young children — I think a bit older than Grace. He might be able to suggest something."

"Excellent idea, love. Let me know what he says."

"You know, Anna, there are times when I feel so weary, as if I have no strength left at all. I don't understand it, for I don't feel ill." Harry stretched his arms and legs. "Ah, that feels better. Perhaps I just need an iron tonic? What do you think?"

"I think that it is time we all had a thorough check-up." Anna took her glasses off and went over and gave him a kiss. "I'll tell you what. As we are moving anyway, why don't we begin by looking for a good doctor's surgery in Golders Green, where we are renting? He might even be able to help with a school, if your boss can't."

"I hate going to the doctors, especially when there doesn't seem to be anything specifically wrong, but perhaps you are right." Harry stood up. "Come, let's go and get some sleep. I don't seem to have had too much of that lately; that affair with Brian really hit me. I don't know what I would have done in his place, but murder, for murder it is, whichever way one looks at it." He shook his head. "It's a difficult burden to carry. We are all guilty, and it seems we have got away with it. The coroner's verdict was that Jones had hanged himself. But the guilt will stay with us forever."

"Try not to think about it, Harry. Let's look towards the future. A brighter future, and hopefully a happier one than these last few months. By the way, have you spoken with Brian lately?"

"No, but I have had Susan on the phone several times, asking me to have a word with him, for it seems he is constantly drunk. What can I say to her? I am not surprised, Susan? So would I be in his place… no, it's no good; all I can do is to tell her to see a doctor, or even a priest. She seems disappointed in me for not having a solution to his problem, but to tell you the truth, I don't even have a solution to my own."

Anna started to put the lights out. "Susan has coped extremely well with the death of Jane. I believe she has constant help from a psychologist, and of course Frederic has been a tremendous help to her. He has turned out to be a very serious, studious young man."

"Thank God for that. I heard he has won a scholarship to Westminster."

"That is true. And the whole family is moving to Chelsea. Susan's mother left her the house in her will. It's a beautiful property in Oakley Street, overlooking Albert Bridge."

"I am happy for them. They deserve it after all their unhappiness."

Early the following year, the Browns moved to Golders Green in London, where they first rented a small flat, but later found their dream home, a stucco-fronted, yellow brick house, set in a quarter of an acre of ground near Kilburn.

After a few years, Harry was promoted to Director of the Poetry Society. Most weeks his poems appeared in some tabloid or another, and there was even talk about a collection of his earlier work being published in a complete volume.

Anna had approached Fortnum and Mason in Piccadilly, London, with samples of her recipes and was now commissioned to bake all their birthday and wedding cakes.

Grace, having attended Lady Eleanor's School for Girls in Hampstead until she was nine, was now in her second year at Mill House. It was a well-established boarding school close to Brighton, where she had made many friends and enjoyed her studies.

In her free time, Grace enjoyed listening to her collection of both classical and modern music on her new CD player, a gift from her parents on her last birthday, whilst pursuing her love of painting and writing. Her greatest joy, however, was to sit under one of the many trees surrounding the school building… the fragile castles in the air of her dreams. Looking at her sitting there with pencil and paper, one could be forgiven for thinking that, at times, she was one in spirit with the great blaze of colours that nature had painted for her.

She learned to listen to nature, playing its tune, even just for a brief moment, before it again would disappear. Birds would hop down and slowly move towards her, only to take to their wings as soon as she stretched her hands out towards them.

"If I can't capture you with my hand, little birds." She laughed. "I will capture you with my pencil in pictures and words." She then quickly drew a scene of them. "I will compose a sonnet for you later, when I am in bed, for now I must get back to my lessons."

She stood up and embraced the old tree trunk, giving it a kiss. "Until tomorrow, my friend. Don't go away." She shook her finger at it, laughing. "And remember, don't shake your leaves too much so they fall down and mess up my painting. Look, what do you think of this bird?" She held the painting of a sparrow up towards the crown of the tree. "Nice, isn't it?"

The tree stood solemn and still, not even moving a leaf.

"All right then, if you don't want to speak to me, I'd better be going, but one day you will talk to me, I promise." She gave it another kiss, then ran quickly back towards the school.

Christmas was now rapidly approaching, and Grace was looking forward to going home for the holiday. She had spent weeks contemplating what to buy everyone. For her mother, it was easy, she was giving her a small tapestry depicting the Virgin and Child, which she had nearly finished. Her teacher had given her many compliments about it, especially the design, which Grace had drawn herself.

Perhaps I will write a story for my father. Yes, that is what I will do. A story about my life here in the school. I will start it tonight. Perhaps I will give him the picture of the sparrow as well. But what can I get for Mr and Mrs Epstein and Frederic? I can't think...

Frederic and his parents had been invited to spend Boxing Day with them, and in her mother's last letter to her, she'd said that the Epsteins, as a thank you gift, had bought tickets for all of them to see Swan Lake, her favourite ballet, at Covent Garden the following day.

Maybe I will get Frederic a small model of a Bugatti. She smiled sadly, remembering their fights. It seemed so long ago now, though just over four years ago. Memories of Jane, sweet little Jane, made tears run down her cheeks.

"I still miss you, I really do," she whispered to the empty room. She went over to her chest of drawers and found a picture of Jane and herself lying on the platform of her unfinished treehouse in Ham, laughing boisterously. The picture was taken by her mother, and had been a constant comfort to her after Jane's untimely death. *I hope, wherever you are, Jane, you are happy now.* She traced her finger slowly over the image, wiping away her tears that had fallen like raindrops onto it, before carefully putting it back.

Later that evening, when Grace was in bed and her three roommates were fast asleep, Grace carefully raised the window blind halfway up, so that the moonlight would give her enough light to write. She was anxious to begin the story for her father. Absentmindedly, she began chewing the end of her pencil, then plumped up the pillows behind her back.

Now, where do I begin? Why is it that the beginning is always so difficult? She spat out a splinter of wood. A torrent of thoughts began running through her head but somehow, she couldn't begin to make sense of them.

All right then! I will start my story by describing this room, which I share with three other girls.

Dear Dad,
Each bed in my dormitory is placed in a corner, and halfway down, between the beds, large wooden wardrobes give each of us, by the sheer size of them, a corner of privacy where we are allowed to keep a few personal things. The head of my bed is facing the large window overlooking the park.
Between my bed and Melissa's, one of my roommates, there is a large chest of drawers, which we share. The two top drawers are mine; the lower ones hers.

My other two roommates, Elsa and Harriet, have their beds facing the door, and each has their own, smaller, chest of drawers. From the tall window I can see the moonlit park, where birch and pine trees grow profusely and where we are allowed to play after our lessons.

As I am lying in my bed, writing this to you, Daddy, I keep looking at the moon as it shines through our uncurtained window. It transforms the bare linoleum floor into a carpet of golden light.

Grace stopped writing. *What a boring beginning*, she thought. *I am not going to write any more tonight.* She turned around to pull the blind down again and was just about to draw a line across her work, when she looked up to see a girl of about her own age, standing in front of her in a short, white, muslin dress. The girl's legs and feet were bare, which surprised her, for it was freezing cold in the dormitory.

Her three roommates were fast asleep, with just the tips of their noses peeping out from beneath their duvets. Their soft breathing was the only thing she could hear in the still room.

"I think you are in the wrong room," Grace whispered. "Are you a new girl? I don't remember seeing you before."

The girl turned around, giggling. Her golden hair, shining in the moonlight, cascaded all the way down to her waist. Her large eyes, like two bright lanterns set in a small, heart-shaped face, were of a colour she had never seen before. They were somehow more blue than blue... or were they green? It was impossible to say.

The girl just stood looking at Grace without speaking.

"I think you had better get back to your own room before Matron finds you wandering about, for then you will be in trouble, and I want to sleep. Goodnight."

Grace turned around and closed her eyes. After a few minutes, she opened them again to see that the girl was still there, sitting gracefully at the end of her bed, looking at her with her beautiful eyes. Suddenly, Grace felt afraid.

"Who are you, and what are you doing in here?"

"I am your teacher," the girl replied with a smile. "I am here to help you recollect the wisdom stored in your subconscious." Her voice was beautiful, soft and musical.

"You have been selected as an experiment, for us to see how it will be possible for the human race to learn again to see, with their inner eye, something that has been forgotten through living in a material world."

Grace sat up, staring at the girl with amazement.

"When you say 'us', who do you mean? Who are 'us'? And how can you be my teacher when you are only my age?" She rubbed her eyes, not quite sure if she was dreaming or not.

"Age has nothing to do with the kind of teacher I am, as you will soon learn." The girl looked down, then continued. "From tomorrow onwards, we begin our lessons. You will never see me again with your visual eyes; my place is in the classroom within yourself. The Old Father of Wisdom, and I, who have been guarding the gifts you took with you to Earth from the room of Earthly treasures, will teach you to recollect — and help you to write a story for your father. There is great need of it, from what I can see." She laughed, pointing to the unfinished writing that had fallen on the floor.

"That sort of thing will take you nowhere. Now you see me as a young girl of your own age, but in reality, I am as old as the universe which created us both. As I said, this is the last time you will see me with your visual eyes. From tomorrow, you will only be able to see me with your inner eye. You will learn to recognise my voice when I teach from within. In other words, I live within you."

"Live within me?" Grace whispered. "I don't understand. Are you mad? How can you live within me?"

The girl stood up, and gently touched Grace's face with a hand as light as moon rays.

"The Old Father of Wisdom and I have always been part of you, but until now, you have not been able to see or hear me. You and I will be like sisters in the classroom. What I teach you from the subconscious, you will direct and make sense of through the conscious mind. And when you are older and understand more of our teachings, you and I will teach the world about a new way of living. Together we will help restore beauty and peace to the world, and perhaps through all of that, humanity might survive. Now I bid you goodnight." She blew Grace a kiss and was gone.

The moon went behind a cloud, leaving the dormitory in darkness.

Grace folded her hands in prayer. "Dear God," she whispered, "the devil has just visited me. Save me, God."

Then, as quick as lightning, she dived under her duvet, totally bewildered. *What was that all about?* She pinched herself hard to again reassure herself that she was fully awake.

A strange new feeling of joy, like a burning current, began running through her whole being. Grace closed her eyes tightly, then immediately saw the girl in her mind's eye. She stood, shaking an old man, who sat in a rocking chair.

"Wake up, Father of Wisdom," the girl called in a voice as sweet as tinkling bells. "Wake up!"

The Old Father of Wisdom opened his eyes, and then stroked his long white beard.

"So you have finally come." His voice was like a running brook. "I never thought it would happen. Have you prepared her?" He pointed his finger at Grace beneath her duvet.

Grace listened as the girl replied, "I have just come from her and have opened her inner eyes and ears. She will be ready for her first lesson."

"In that case, I have much to prepare." He stood up and lit his pipe. "Am I to understand that she remembers nothing of her previous teaching?" The Old Father of Wisdom's eyes seemed to look right through Grace, as he shook his head.

"Nothing at all." The girl went to him and kissed his cheek. "Nothing as yet, that is, but she will recall everything through me, and I will at all times be protecting her from the long-ago evil vapours."

What evil vapours? thought Grace, who was still listening. The girl saw Grace looking at her.

"Go to sleep now," she whispered, closing her inner eyes and ears gently. "You will have a busy day tomorrow."

Grace fell asleep. Sleeping the sleep of the innocent child that she was, she began dreaming. She dreamt that she was sitting next to the golden girl in a large classroom, where the Old Father of Wisdom stood at the blackboard, writing some strange, unrecognisable sentences.

What am I doing here? she wondered.

Then the voice of the old master rang through the room. "Small wonder the world is in the state in which it finds itself," he began, giving them a penetrating look. "Take out your papers and begin writing!" he bellowed.

"Where are the papers and pen?" Grace whispered to the girl, as she opened her empty desk.

"It is not a pen you write with, but your subconscious thoughts," the girl whispered back. "Just think that you are writing. It will reach your conscious mind. In time, it will open the door to your inner self."

"I will try." Grace closed her eyes and imagined she was writing.

The Master of Wisdom continued adjusting his glasses. "I see how easily the mind can doubt the greatness of the power of the living word." He pointed towards them. "By the end of this century, I will move on to the highest level of consciousness, close to the infinite Creator. And it is hoped that, with everything you have learned from me by then, both of you will join me there."

What is he talking about? Grace thought. *What is the higher level of consciousness?* She shook her head. *I don't believe a word he is saying.*

"Concentrate, child." His voice held the venom of vipers.

With some reluctance, Grace tried to block out her conscious thoughts, and listen to what he was saying.

"You..." He pointed to her, "must allow the changes to take place within yourself. Concentrate on the teaching available to you, spiritually and morally. Grow into that which has been part of your world since the beginning of time."

Grace tried to concentrate, though she still found it difficult to understand what he was talking about.

"Sadly, I feel a weakness in you..." Again, he looked at Grace with his penetrating eyes.

He can read my mind too; I had better be careful what I think. Grace lowered her head.

"...which was not present before." His voice, though kinder now, touched her with such a force that she almost fell off the chair.

Before when? Grace was totally lost. *Could it be that age has something to do with it?*

His voice cut through her thoughts. "Age, as has been said a million times before, is relative to that which it touches."

Grace looked at the golden girl, sitting smiling next to her, remembering what she had said the night before, when she had told her that she was as old as the universe itself.

"Yes, I know," the voice agreed, "it is not easy to grasp. What I meant was that age is of all ages. Correction… age has no meaning as age itself. It is a sleeping torrent that dominates your very being, by dictating and regulating the organized system within your conscious body. A child of one can be older than a man of ninety and vice versa. Age itself has nothing to do with man, only with the deterioration of the working parts of the internal organs of that same body structure surrounding the living, growing spirit within. Man is, in essence, the living spirit."

The golden girl took Grace's hand, and then whispered, "It is true. But listen carefully. It will be interesting now."

Grace nodded her head, giving her a smile as she did her best to concentrate on what was said.

"Why can you not understand, that the slow human mind…"

Grace looked at him, surprised.

"Yes, I said slow mind can absorb nothing, unless we, the creative force all around, allow that to happen. I have said this a million times before, to as many students, and now I say it again to you. There is no difference between you and me."

You are wrong, old man, thought Grace. *I am a young girl of nearly thirteen, and you are an old man. What do you mean 'there is no difference'?* She yawned.

Suddenly, she felt an electric shock seize her. She looked up, and saw the Old Father of Wisdom standing in front of her.

"As I said... and this time, pay attention... in reality, we are all the same, but as we are separated by different levels of awareness, so are we also different in size and shape.

"Where I am teaching from at this very moment, I perceive everything below, but nothing above." He gave Grace a penetrating look. "You have the added bonus of being able to communicate with that above you, due to our intervention long ago. Remember what you said?"

Grace shook her head, then whispered to the golden girl, "You are right, this is getting interesting, and I think I am beginning to understand."

"I knew you were ready," the girl whispered back. "Just listen."

"But now I suppose that is one of the things you are going to tell me you have forgotten, too." The old man turned around and walked back to the blackboard, then faced her again, before continuing.

"Let me remind you..." he stretched his arms wide as his voice rose like a powerful wave, "...you said 'I shall go to the world below. I will take on the mantle of human form and be the teacher they have been waiting for. Not the son of the divine, but a being like themselves who will know, like them, of the struggle for survival, the pain and joy of mortal life. I will go and teach them to be free, liberated, so that neither age nor mind will destroy that divinity within'." Here, the old father stopped to write something on the blackboard, which looked like Mind.

"I will remind you that you said 'mind' and rightly so, but that is not to discriminate against that wonder of central function in your head, but to remind you that it is not with the mind that man lives. It is through the living spirit only, as you should also remember, for your first teachings were by the Creator himself. These were his words…" The Master's voice rose by an octave. "Everything that lives, is created by me," God said. "Everything else, by man. Child, must I remind you which is the greatest? That which cannot die, or that which is always dead? Surely you cannot have forgotten those words through your short stay on the Earth plane?"

The Master walked towards Grace as he continued. "Awaken, child. The time has come for you to participate in the greatness of the unfolding of the next stage of man's development. Robust and strong, you will be standing next to and close to the centre of all that will happen. Living, yet dead, as the spirit bursts into flames and sends its light up into the realm from where it came.

"A thousand miles of hard walking seems to have taken you nowhere. Can it be that too much has been given, so that contentment in a physical world starts to override the greatness within? I hope not, for in that case, work to eliminate those layers will have to start immediately, and I, myself, as your former guide and now your teacher, will have to be the one who removes them. I say former guide, but that does not mean that I am no longer… I am only referring to the time when you, as a small child, sat in my class.

"The most attentive of my students, you absorbed everything you were taught, growing in spirit so rapidly that, within a short time, you were as I, eliminating the light from a fully developed spirit. Trusting nothing but that burning flame as it spread its light over that which had been in darkness and despair.

"Holy, holy, is that light that burns away within its flame the impure and rejuvenates the old so that, though the body fades and folds, the living flame consumes and spreads like a glorious flower throughout the body. Unfolding layers of impurities will melt away as the divine flame spreads its golden river through every fibre of the body until all is absorbed. Then falls away as the liberated spirit rises towards the heavenly powers again."

The Old Father of Wisdom turned his back, and then he was gone.

All Grace could think was, *Does he always speak like this?* Then she woke up.

Chapter 14

The next morning Grace was called into the matron's study.

"Grace, my dear, sit down." Matron looked seriously over her half-moon glasses perched on her pointed nose. She pointed to a chair in front of her desk. "I am afraid…" She placed both hands firmly in front of her on the old oak desk as if to steady herself. "I have some bad news for you. Your mother has just phoned to ask me to tell you that your father is seriously ill in hospital. You are to leave immediately. As soon as you are ready, Thomas will drive you to the station and purchase your ticket to St. Pancras, where your mother will be waiting for you."

Grace felt faint and began shaking all over, but managed to stand up and curtsey. "Thank you, Matron, I will go and pack now." She bit her bottom lip so hard she tasted blood.

"I am so sorry, my dear." Matron stood up and shook her hand. "Let me know how you get on, and we shall look forward to seeing you back here after the Christmas break."

Grace wanted to wish Matron a happy Christmas, but somehow she just couldn't get the words out.

"God bless you, child, and give my deepest respect to your mother."

Once out of Matron's study, Grace raced up the stairs, with tears streaming down her face. She quickly threw a few things into her battered suitcase and wrote a note to her roommates, telling them what had happened.

About two hours later, the train pulled into St Pancras Station, London. Grace looked out of the window and saw her mother standing, with a blue scarf around her head, looking anxiously towards the carriage doors as they opened.

"Mum! Mum!" Grace shouted, as she ran into her mother's outstretched arms. "Oh, Mum! How is Dad? He will be all right, won't he?" she pleaded in a small, tearful voice.

Anna held her tight, as she spoke through muffled sobs.

"I'm afraid not, my darling girl. He died just over an hour ago. It was very quick, I never even…" she began to sob loudly. "…had time to say goodbye."

"No, Mum. No! Don't say that. It can't be true. I want to see him. I wrote a story for him for Christmas, I want to read it to him… *now*!" Grace's anguished voice rose until she finished up shouting.

"Come, my darling, don't let us stay here in the cold." Anna wiped her tears. "I have a cab waiting that will take us to St Thomas' hospital, where your father is lying."

Both were crying hysterically as they entered the cab. Fifteen minutes later, they arrived at the hospital.

"That won't be necessary, madam," the taxi driver said, shaking his head when Anna handed him the fare. "I hope everything turns out all right, madam." He touched his cap before driving off.

A nurse took them up to the small, private, pale green room where Harry Brown lay, peacefully, as if asleep.

"If there is anything I can do for you, Mrs Brown, just press there." The young nurse pointed to a small red button at the end of the bed, then quietly left the room.

Grace ran over and took her father's cold hand in her own.

"Dad! Dad! Oh, why did you have to die? Please, Dad, I wrote a story for you. Please, Dad, wake up, I want you to hear it."

As Grace fumbled in her bag, her purse fell out, spilling coins on the floor. Then she pulled out the crumpled piece of paper. "Please listen, Dad, I wrote it for you."

She started to read aloud between sobs.

Thoughts

What are these thoughts stumbling... waiting to be known? Could it be that long ago I knew them only too well?

I reach out to be in touch, only to find that they slip through my mind, leaving not only a space uncluttered and bare but also an emptiness like a gaping soul unfulfilled within itself. I am struggling to understand, but cannot begin to connect my mind with the vast void, the pearls from the depths...

I feel so still, so empty, like the still wind as it dances across the ocean waves... leaving them as they were, without creating even a single wave apart from themselves.

What shall I do, as I sit here like the shell of the living no longer being felt?

What shall I do, as all around me tears and laughter are being heard from another shore, awakening into this reality, sampling the fruits, and bringing me closer to the living than the living themselves?

No longer alone in the essence we know, for the land beyond the shore stretches far and wide, and as I walk forward into that land, I leave behind the shadows of yesterday and unburden myself of the litter carried in that empty space.

No longer can I hope that I may be understood, for indeed how can anyone understand the longing for that which is not known... or known as we know it to be?

As I walk forward, my foot is no longer unsure, no longer walking with a heavy tread but moving with a power greater than the one which is keeping me alive, for indeed it is a life — though different from the life I am surrounded by.

I no longer pursue the pleasures of the senses.

I feel as empty as the little shell on the beach after the bird alighted on its fruit.

Could it be that a new beginning is about to unfold itself to me, and can it be that I shall grow in this new existence?

I, for one, do not hesitate to go forward into this new awareness. I do not tarry nor wait at the door, but bring the house down in order to enter. Can my life be as altered as that, I ask myself... since yesterday was as the days before?

Can it be, that in a short space of time, when we sample the fruit of the other vine, then nothing matters any more?

Come, child of the human race, hold my hand and walk with me into the land beyond, where thirst and cold will no longer be felt, for there will be no need of such. Walk, child, into the land above. Hold my hand so as not to get lost. Do not be afraid of the current taking us there.

(I can no longer feel my human form. It is like a shell left behind, though I know myself enough to sit here at the table writing this.)

What is the purpose of this journey of mine into the unknown? What will I find beyond the closed door? Do I go, trusting as a child into that bowl, which can hold perhaps only a tiny fish? Will I be confined there for as long as they — or I — like? I have to trust as the hand reaches out, and we move forward into a great, enveloping mist.

The mist is clearing. Beyond are colours never seen here on Earth. The colours are living things, they are waiting to greet the colour which each one is allocated on Earth. Mine is some shade of blue. It twists and turns and totally surrounds me, as it lifts me up into the space above.

The colour has done its job. I am left in a space where there is nothing but light.

Suddenly a being comes towards me, a being of such beauty that I find it difficult to comprehend. The being advances and says, 'Soon it will be time to go... and I shall return again, for the forces on Earth are such now, that I can safely follow the pattern of that journey. Fear not, child, for that which you have created has grown into a powerful thing and awaits its coming.

"Child, be not despondent about all the mishaps, which have been outside your control, but prepare in body and mind for the coming of the light. See how the passage has been cleared, as it was two thousand years ago, by the star terminating the vapours of evil forces, which had risen up above the current to be used."

(The being is now in front of me. Never did I see such light... It looks like he... he looks like one who is encrusted with many shining jewels, but no form or shape of such is to be seen.)

The being continues speaking. His voice is so powerful, I nearly fall backwards as he says,

'I come on the night when the ocean turns the sky.
I come when the mountains lay down their fires.

I come when the blossom begins to fall.
I await the final and ultimate demand,
Then I shall come as a glorious star.

I bring with me not disaster and death... but the living light to the mindless death.

I bring with me a vase *containing the flower whose beauty will bring new life.*

I reach out to the ones believing in me — bringing them to the ultimate light — before judging to which stable they belong.

I have not come to waste my time, no more measures of tidings for the human race — I have brought songs, as I strip the life at evening tide. Then lift the one who believes to the light of my top.'

I am standing alone — the being turns his back — and walks the other way — the colour of blue brings me back in my body again.'

"Oh, Dad, Dad!" she shouted, prostrating herself over the cold body, as if by her own warmth and strength, it would come alive again.

Anna stood in the doorway, tears streaming down her face, then she walked over and lifted Grace away from her father.

"Leave me alone, Mum," she shouted. "Don't touch me!" She lashed out at her.

"Grace, stop it." Anna took hold of her arm. "That was a beautiful story, dear. I am sure your father was able to hear it, wherever he is." She stroked the still, cold face of her beloved husband.

"Sleep in peace, my darling, and send us your love from your new life, until we are together again." She bent down, kissing his cold lips, and for a split second, Grace imagined that her father smiled.

Later, she learned from the doctors that such things often happen, due to contractions of muscles, nerves and tissues.

"Come, my dearest, let us go, and let your father rest in peace. He is somewhere now writing us beautiful poems which he will find a way to send to us. Perhaps through the touch of the summer wind on our skin or through the sound of the pebbles washed by the clear river waters, or in the humming of a bumblebee. We must learn to listen. Life is so full of mysteries."

"I know he will, Mum, and when he does, I will listen, and catch them and then write them down for you."

"Do that. That is the greatest gift we can give to each other. His respect, and trust, the treasures of our joint love, these are the gifts he has left us, and with those gifts, we will continue to make our life rich, in spite of this devastating sadness tearing our hearts apart."

Anna touched Grace's cheeks gently before wiping her tears. Then she opened her handbag and took out a small, hardback book.

"This is for you, darling. Your father dedicated his new and last volume of poems to you, as an early Christmas present. Take it with you to your room when we get back, read it, and feel the closeness of his love, for each word, each sentence, comes from his heart to you."

At home, Anna took off her hat and coat and then helped Grace with hers. "I am going to lie down and try to get some rest, for I have not slept for the last three days."

Grace kissed the book and then ran up to her room, throwing herself on her bed, sobbing as if her heart was breaking. The day turned into night and she had not stirred. She was still lying on her stomach across the bed, fast asleep, her feet dangling near the floor. The house was still. Anna had taken the receiver off the hook before retiring to her room with her private thoughts.

When Grace finally woke up, it was bright sunlight, but freezing cold in her room. Her hands felt numb from sleeping on them, and her feet were like two frozen blocks of ice. She sat up slowly, and for a moment imagined it was all a bad dream, then the realization hit her like a stabbing pain in her chest. She walked over to wash her tear-stained face in the sink, then tiptoed downstairs, listening to the silence of her mother's room as she passed.

In the kitchen, the cleaner had left a cold supper on a tray the day before. She looked at it with disquiet and tipped it into the bin, before putting the kettle on to make tea. She opened the fridge, found a carton of orange juice and poured herself a glass.

Her father's pipe was lying in the ashtray on the breakfast table. Grace picked it up, then held it to her nose and smelled the tobacco aroma. Memories flooded back, and tears again began to flow down her cheeks. She took the tea towel and dried her face and blew her nose in it, then carefully lit the pipe and sucked in the smoke. She coughed and spluttered violently.

"Grace, whatever are you doing?" Her mother stood in her dressing gown in the doorway. "Put that pipe down, this instant."

Grace put it down, and then ran into her mother's arms, as the tobacco aroma wrapped itself around them.

"Oh, Mum! Mum! What are we to do? I can't live without Dad. I can't," she sobbed.

"We must, darling. Let us try to be brave. For that is what your father would have wanted. Let us show him that all the wonderful qualities he has left us with are not wasted. We will carry on in the knowledge that he loved us and in knowing that that love will never die, but unfold like a flower, spreading its seeds to make others grow.

"We are very privileged, for we carry his love within our hearts, and that is something that will never die. Now, child, we have many things to get on with. Hanna should be here soon, and friends will want to come to pay their respects, so let us put the receiver back on the telephone and greet them with the love they deserve."

"I can't, Mum. I just can't! I feel so awful, I can't," Grace sobbed.

"I know, dear." Anna kissed her cheeks. "But we must. It is what your father would have wanted. We have to be brave and go through this together."

"Oh, Mum! Mum, I feel sick." Grace ran over to the sink and threw up the orange juice.

"Grace, I am so sorry. Come, let us go upstairs and get cleaned up."

Anna went over and turned the thermostat up on the old heater. The doorbell rang, and then a key turned in the lock and Hanna, their daily help, walked in with red, swollen eyes. Her unbrushed hair curled in wisps around her face. She blew her nose into a crumpled hanky, stamping her feet to get her circulation working after the intense cold from outside.

She took off her long brown coat before walking over to give Anna a hug.

"I am so sorry, madam, and little Grace too… what a shock. My insides turned over when I heard… and it was so sudden! I thought the gentleman had only caught a cold, and now he is gone." She began sniffing, then blew her nose loudly again before taking off her rubber boots and putting on a pair of checked indoor slippers.

"I will go and see to things in the kitchen and take telephone messages for you, madam. Just you go upstairs and rest." Still blowing her nose, Hanna squeezed her ample shape through the doorway into the kitchen.

Chapter 15

Christmas came and went with very little in the way of celebration in the Brown household. Frederic and his parents stayed for a few days and, as planned, they all went to see Swan Lake at Covent Garden with Margot Fontaine dancing the lead.

Condolences arrived in the form of letters, phone calls and visitors. It was all very sad.

Frederic had grown into a tall, slim youth of seventeen and was seriously studying music.

"When I am finished with my A levels." He grinned. "I have got a place at the Music Conservatoire at Marylebone Road. I can't wait. I have already had some success with a few small pieces I have composed for a French ballet. Have you heard of 'La Socorro' by Mullah?" he asked her.

Grace shook her head sadly; all she could think of was her father.

"We didn't know his heart was damaged. Mum said he refused to go and see a doctor, that he was only tired. Oh! If only he had, then he might still be here now."

"It is no good thinking what might have been. Just remember the good times you had together." Frederic reached for her hand.

"I know. I am trying, but it is so difficult."

"I'll tell you what, Grace. When the opera has its opening night in the spring, I will send you and your mother a ticket, would you like that?"

"Thank you, Frederic." She sniffed. "That would be very special."

"Your pain will get less over the years, Grace, I know. When I think of Jane, and how badly I treated her at times, I can't forgive myself."

"We were all silly. But you were horrible at times." Grace gave him a tearful smile.

"I used to call you a little monster." Frederic shook his head.

"And I called you 'that stupid boy', but I didn't really mean it."

They hugged each other.

"Thank you for coming, Frederic; it can't have been a very happy Christmas for you and your parents."

"I am glad we did. Friends should be there for each other. I remember how kind and helpful you all were when Jane died. My father always said that had it not been for your father, things might have turned out very differently. But he never really explained what he meant by that."

"Sometimes adults are more complex than children. Perhaps it is better not to try to understand them." Grace smiled through her tears.

"We are going back to Chelsea later today. If you feel like it, why don't you come with us? We could go and see a film in the afternoon. They are showing Dickens' *A Christmas Carol* at the ABC in Fulham Road. But I don't suppose you're allowed to go out alone in the evening?"

"No, I am not. Mum says I will have to wait until I am fourteen, in the spring. Anyway, I don't feel like going anywhere, and Mum needs me here. But thank you all the same, you are very kind." She gave him a hug. "I'll tell you what, though. In a few weeks' time, before I go back to school, I am coming to Chelsea to buy my new sports kit at Peter Jones. Perhaps we could meet there and have a Coke together? Mum will be with me, but we could always send her to have her hair done." Grace laughed now. "She needs it, too... only yesterday she asked me to cut her fringe, and what a mess I made of it!"

Frederic laughed too. "I thought it looked a bit strange, but I put it down to a new fashion. That is a great idea, Grace, I look forward to seeing you then. Give me a call and let me know when you are finished shopping."

"I will. Bye, Frederic." She kissed his cheek. "Enjoy the film."

Anna gave Grace a big hug after everyone had gone. "Now there is just you and me left in our family. Come, let us go and relax with a cool drink. I am exhausted."

"Mum? What happened to Dad's real parents? Did he ever find out?"

"No. Your father was reluctant to talk about his background, but he believed they were dead. He was only three months old when he was adopted by Mr and Mrs Brown. Your father once told me that his adoptive parents never talked about his background, only that he came from Germany, and that his real parents had died. But you already know that. Why are you asking?"

"I don't know, Mum. Perhaps it's to try to find out as much as I can about Dad now that he is gone. There will be nothing new to share."

"Perhaps not. But we have our memories of all the years together. That should be enough for a lifetime… don't you think?"

"I know." Grace poured a glass of lemonade from a carton and drank it. "Do you want one, Mum?"

"No, thank you. I think I will have a glass of wine with some of these delicious chocolates that Susan and Brian brought us. They have become such good friends, and Frederic — such a studious young man — and so handsome." She laughed as Grace blushed.

"I couldn't help hearing you talking about meeting him in Chelsea when we go to Peter Jones. That will be nice for you both — and you are right, I do need a haircut — badly. I would advise you never to take up hairdressing!" She chuckled.

The holiday was soon over, and Grace went back to her boarding school, where she stayed until she was eighteen. Then she was offered a place at Cambridge to study English, German and Philosophy.

Grace never doubted what she wanted to do after graduation. She planned to stay on to get her master's degree, then look for a place within higher education, teaching philosophy.

After her father's death, her mother had let her take as many of his books and manuscripts as she wanted. Among them was an old folder she had found tucked away behind a row of books on one of the top shelves, containing letters and documents written in Austrian German. At the time, Grace had put the folder away in her cupboard, knowing that her German was not good enough to understand the writing and also, it felt like prying, as they looked like they were mostly private letters.

Now, years later at Cambridge, she came across them again whilst tidying her shelves.

Why am I keeping them? she wondered. *I will have to either throw them out, or translate them. Let me translate them, it will be a good exercise. After all, it can't hurt anyone now that Dad has been dead for more than five years.*

Grace sat down at her desk and spread the letters and papers out. The first document she opened was written by a seventeen-year-old Jewish girl from Vienna, by the name of, Sarah Kirchstein. In small, tight handwriting, it began:

Love is a beautiful but strange thing...

When I think how it happened to me, a well brought up Jewish girl, living a quiet life with my parents at Rodale Gardens, one of Vienna's most expensive districts... I can only shake my head in wonder.

My father is a respectable City banker, and my loving mother, one of the town's celebrated beauties, is always involved with numerous charities.

How could Cupid's arrow pierce me so violently? That I was prepared to do anything... anything to be with my love, that poor starving boy I had watched shovelling snow in front of our house for months.

I was at home resting in my room on the morning of that fateful day in 1926, when my whole life changed. My usual music lesson with Miss Cousting had been cancelled due to my mild cold. Rabbi Elijah was arriving later, to share the evening of Atonement with us. I was instructed to entertain him if he was to come before my dear mother was back from visiting some distant relatives at the other end of town.

My mother had just stepped out of the house and was walking towards the horse-drawn sledge, where Fritz, our chauffeur, stood holding the door open for her. Suddenly I heard her give a loud cry. I ran to the window and saw Fritz gesturing wildly to our maid, standing in the doorway, to come and help my mother back into the house.

Then he bent down and tried to get the young, dark-haired street cleaner, who had collapsed and lay prostrate in the snow, to sit up.

My mother, dressed in rich fur, took a few steps backwards, and her feet sank into a deep pile of snow the street cleaner had brushed together. She looked down at her beautiful hand-sewn shoes. They were completely ruined. Then, with the help of Olga, her maid, she went back into the house.

Fritz tethered the horses, which stood stamping their hooves and raring to go, their hot breath rising like smoke in the cold morning frost. Then he ran back to the young man, and after some attempts, managed to pull him into the house, where he urged Frau Heinz, the housekeeper, to phone for the doctor. He then carefully laid him on one of the kitchen benches, before returning to the horses.

By this time, I had run down the stairs, and stood peeping into the kitchen from behind the door. I watched Cook wrapping a blanket around the shivering youth. Carla, the kitchen maid, stood with her mouth open as if she was in need of more air in order to think.

Cook snapped at her. "Don't stand there gawping, girl, make a hot drink for the lad." Then she went over to see if she could wake him.

The young man, looking like he was in shock, started to shake violently. Carla brought the hot tea laced with sugar and milk, which Cook tried to get him to drink, whilst holding his head up.

He opened his dark penetrating eyes of a colour not unlike a stormy sea when at its coldest… then closed them again, as if the light hurt them. The smell of the oil lamp hanging from the ceiling made him sick. He tried to sit up, only to fall backwards again.

Cook kindly cleaned him up, and then managed to get some of the warm tea down his throat. After a while, his shivering stopped. His clothes were soaked from the early morning rain, and his black hair fell in long, unkempt strands over his forehead.

"Where am I?" he muttered, as he looked around the cosy kitchen.

Cook brought over a towel and started to rub his hair. "Hello, young man," she said cheerfully. "I am glad to see you have come round. For a moment, I thought you were a goner."

"Where am I?" he whispered again.

"You are in Master Kirchstein the elder's, house. Fritz, the chauffeur, brought you in after you fainted in the snow. What is your name, lad?" she asked kindly.

"Adolph." He tried to smile, but it came across as a grimace.

Cook went over to stir a pot roast, cooking on the fire. The lid rattled as she took it off, then put it down on the sideboard. A delicious smell of stew wafted through the kitchen. Carla went back to chop vegetables, her wooden clogs just peeping out from under her long black skirt with her coarse white blouse tucked into its waistband. She looked at Adolph from beneath long black eyelashes.

Cook wiped the sweat from her forehead with an old rag, and then brushed her long white apron down.

"You look mighty hungry to me, lad." She handed him a bowl of hot soup.

Adolph took a few careful spoonsful, then laid the spoon down before lifting the bowl to his lips, drinking voraciously whilst using his fingers to eat the solid pieces.

"No gracious manners about you," Cook laughed. "But no matter, the important thing is that it stays down."

Adolph ignored her after finishing the soup, and buttoned his dirty jacket before pulling the collar up around his face as if to hide himself. He then lay down, closing his eyes.

"That's all right, lad, you just rest awhile," she said good-humouredly as, grinning broadly, she removed the empty bowl.

The sunlight was streaming in through the window. Cook was back at her table working a batch of bread dough. Her stout arms moved rapidly as she kneaded it with her closed fists. Suddenly, I heard my mother's footsteps on the stairs. Quick as a flash, I ran into the pantry and half-closed the door.

Carla, who had stopped chopping, went over to take her coat.

"How is the young man?" My mother's voice was soft and full of concern. "He gave me quite a shock, out there." She looked at the youth, lying pale as death with his arms dangling towards the floor.

"Coming to, my lady." Cook smiled. *"No injuries. Pure starvation, I should say. With a bit of food down his skinny neck, he will soon be right again."*

"I am glad to hear that." My mother started to leave. *"The doctor is unable to come; he has been called out to an emergency... a birth, I believe.'*

"Don't worry my lady. When he comes round again, we will get him to take some more broth. That should put him back on his legs.'

My mother left, closing the door after her.

After standing for a few minutes in the pantry, I decided not to be so silly, and go into the kitchen myself to enquire about the man.

Adolph could hear what they were saying, but kept his eyes tightly closed and thought, I might as well stay here for as long as I can, than being out there shovelling that shit — *then he uttered a weak cry, just as I stepped into the kitchen.*

"Oh dear, he seems to be in pain, Cook!" I ran to his side.

"Hunger pain, Miss Sarah." Cook patted her round stomach. *"But what are we to do with him, Miss? He can't stay here the whole day."*

"Let him stay here for a while, then see if you can get him to eat something. And I will find some of my

father's old clothes for him, he looks totally frozen in those thin rags. And look at his shoes, there are hardly any soles left on them." I bent down and had a closer look at him, then turned to Carla.

"Please bring me a towel, his hair is soaking wet.'

Adolph looked at me from the corner of one eye. He thought to himself, you can look, my lovely lady, and maybe one-day I shall take a good look at you. *He opened his eyes and looked straight into mine as I bent down to dry his hair. I blushed, and then handed the towel to Cook before leaving the kitchen. My footsteps sounded like drumbeats as I ran rapidly up the wooden stairs.*

Cook looked at Carla with a knowing smile. "I do believe that the young miss has taken a fancy to the lad."

Adolph smiled as he thought, Yes… that one will be an easy lay — just you wait, lady. *He was now fully awake, only pretending to be asleep so as to prolong his stay in the warm kitchen.*

Later that morning, I went down to the kitchen again with some of my father's old clothes, which I gave to Cook.

"Please give these to him before he leaves," I said.

"That is very kind of you, miss." She laid the clothes down on a chair.

In readiness for our guest, I had changed into a beautiful red velvet cloak, trimmed with white ermine, and beneath it I wore my new yellow silk dress. My maid had arranged my hair in a fashionable style of tight curls hanging around my face. And on my feet I wore my new black pumps.

The young man was asleep, and Cook told me that there was no need to worry; he had just finished a bowl of her soup. I looked at his starved, pale face, noting how his cheekbones protruded sharply, and at the mass of black hair falling over his forehead. I wondered what had happened to him; why he was reduced to cleaning the streets. In spite of his condition, he looked much too intelligent for that.

Adolph must have sensed that I was studying him again, for he opened his eyes and looked straight into mine, then smiled. And that was that. Our fate was sealed. I was in love. Blushing, I ran out of the kitchen, catching the sound of his soft laughter behind me.

And that is really where Adolph's and my story began and ended. Our love was later sealed with my pregnancy, and then came our separation and the cessation of life with my family... but let me go on and tell the story — as Adolph himself told it to me.

Adolph sat up, then slowly got to his feet.

"Well done, lad." Cook came running over. "Fit for the outside again. Here, take this with you." She handed him a large chunk of bread and a lump of cheese.

"Ma'am, I am most profoundly grateful for all your help." He bowed, mockingly, thinking, you silly old

cow, I don't give a damn for you or your goddamn food. Oh, Christ, how I long for power, for then I will show all you stuck up, fat-arsed yes and no people, who I really am. And that doe-eyed young bitch in all her silk and velvets, who looked at me as if I were some sort of curiosity in a circus, I will show you too, just you wait. But now, I must get back to shovelling snow, or I shall get the sack.

Adolph took a few unsteady steps.

"Don't forget the clothes. Miss Sarah brought you these." Carla handed him the clothes. "She was most insistent that we gave them to you. I hope they fit."

Adolph took the clothes from her, and gave her a big grin, showing white, irregular teeth. He quickly changed into the heavy, military coat, then pulled on the strong black boots. He felt inclined to take the coat off again, since the military bastards did not want him in the army. What was it they had said? Too frail to even carry a gun. They had laughed as they showed him the door. The bastards must have been out there slaughtering a few decent people, so why should he advertise their shit? Then he thought better of it as he remembered it was bitterly cold outside.

He mockingly thanked the cook and Carla again for their kindness, then went up the steps to the back door. The door stuck as he tried to push it open. The wind howled as huge snowdrifts piled up at the back and front of the house. Damn it all, I have only just cleared this pathway and now it is totally covered again, *he thought.*

He picked up his shovel, which Fritz had leaned against the back gate, and then began shovelling, but after a few minutes he was too exhausted to do any more, and as it was starting to get dark, he decided to go back to the doss house where he had lived for the past six months.

Sarah had stood at her window, watching him. He waved to her. She smiled back.

"I am going to get to know that young lady, if I know anything. But how do I go about it?"

"You follow my advice."

Adolph swung round to see who was speaking, and there behind him stood a near-naked youth. His blond hair was brushed neatly away from his forehead, allowing two piercing dark eyes to penetrate his gaze, almost hypnotically.

"Oh, and a fat lot of good that will do me, looking at the way you are dressed, mate! You won't last long in this cold." He looked up at the heavy snow clouds gathered overhead. "But what exactly do you mean by following your advice?"

The youth laughed. "It is you that won't last long being here on the street, in spite of your heavy coat, for your body is starved of nutrition. I, on the other hand, need neither clothes nor food, for my survival. All I need is your body to house me."

"My body to house you?" Adolph leaned heavily on his shovel. "What do you mean by that?'

"I mean," replied the stranger, *"that when we are alone, you will be able to see me, but when others are around, I will merge myself with you. Quite simple."*

"It might seem simple to you, mate," Adolph started to walk in the direction of the doss house, *"but to me, you seem stark raving mad. How can you merge with me?'*

"Like this." Suddenly the stranger disappeared and Adolph felt, within, a sensation of being stuffed with soft cushions, if that were possible. Then the stranger was back again, grinning broadly.

"Are you saying," Adolph looked at the stranger curiously, *"that you can, at any time, be part of me?'*

"That's about it! I have just demonstrated it. It is the easiest thing in the world."

Adolph was about to say something sarcastic, but instead asked, *"What do you want?"* He looked at the grinning youth. *"What is the purpose of all this?'*

"The purpose is power. You have called on me many a time. So here I am."

"I have never called on you. I don't know you, so move your arse and let me get home." He tried to push the youth to the side but found his hand going straight through him.

"Not so fast, young man. You do know me. We met before you were born. You chose power as your gift to take with you to Earth, there have been many times, whilst dormant within you. I have listened to you calling my name, when loneliness bit into you and

disappointment left your soul crying for justice. You called on me when the elders took away your dying father and when your mother sneaked out to visit the merchant down the road, leaving you, a small lad, crying in his bed. You have called on me a thousand times."

"God damn you! How did you know about my mother, that bitch?'

"I know everything about your life. I have been part of you since before birth. You remember, or shall I remind you, lying in your little bed with your fists tightly closed, screaming, "If only I had power, I would squash that fat merchant!" A thousand times I have heard you in different situations, calling on me... as recent as today! Well, my friend, you do have powers. They were always part of you. But you, yourself, will have to recollect, and bring to life that which you are. And now that we have met, let me tell you how to make the most of it, for there are many types of power."

"I don't believe a word of that rubbish you are dishing out. I can only think I am having some sort of hallucination. But just for the hell of it, let us say you are who you say you are. In that case, I want enough power to rule the world, and I want to start by eliminating all the pompous Jewish arses, who don't give a damn for anyone but themselves and their own people."

"That is a tall order. Do you know how many Jews there are in the world today?'

"Got no idea, mate, but the bastards seem to be everywhere to stop me doing what I want to do. I don't give a damn about them. They are pests — no better than vermin, every one of them. Did any of them ever, ever, stand by me with any help or support? Except perhaps today... I also want to have the biggest and most valued art collection in the world, as I was even denied the chance to study art, and guess by whom?"

"I cannot."

"A Jew. A rotten, stinking Jew!'

"You are suggesting some hair-raising proposals. The paintings you are thinking about, are they not mostly housed in museums and private collections?"

"That's right. So, in that case, I will just have to have enough power to steal them. Isn't that where you come in?"

"As you wish."

"Will I have any regrets?"

"None whatsoever, for I will take this *as payment for my services."*

"What is that?"

The stranger held a round mass, the size of a tennis ball, in his hand. "Your soul. For that is something you will have no use for any more, and with that, your conscience will go, too."

"Great! But where do I begin?" Adolph kicked the snow with his new boots.

"You have already begun. But I can see that you have left a powerful image in the heart of that young

lady in there." The stranger pointed to the mansion. "It will be an easy thing to get her to follow you. When you go there tomorrow to shovel the snow, wait for her parents to go out, then ring the bell and demand to speak with her. Say you want to thank her personally for her kindness to you yesterday."

"Kindness," Adolph sneered. "The bitch only gave away what no one else wanted."

"True, but don't let her know that. And from there on, I will guide you as to what you do, and where you go."

"You mean I shall be leaving?"

"Oh, yes. You will be going over the border into Germany, to join the army there."

"But God damn it! They will have nothing to do with me."

"I told you, I will lead you. Just go there and say you want to join up, but first finish what you intend to do with that young lady."

"That, my dear chap, will be my greatest pleasure."

The stranger laughed. "And mine, too. Don't forget we are part of one another."

"In that case, do I always have to listen to what you tell me?"

"Yes, but it happens from within. You will never know it is from me. Within the next half an hour you will have forgotten all about me, as you see me here. Instead, you will be filled with an uncontrollable power

that will enable you to achieve all your desires. Before I fade from your mind, let me just tell you one more thing:

"There will be people who want to use you for experimenting with deadly gases such as mustard gas and so forth. You, yourself, will be personally experimented on with a new drug intended to empower the mind of man, but beware, for they can, and will, at the end eliminate you, too. We will meet again." The stranger quickly merged with him.

"Hey! Wait a moment. You can't just come here and tell me a pack of lies and then disappear! Come back out here again!" Adolph hammered on his chest with his closed fists.

"What do you want?" The stranger spoke from within.

"I want to know how the hell this all came about? You told me it was before my birth. It doesn't make sense to me."

"Sense with your conscious mind, no. But you have within your subconscious the ultimate powers for total destruction, including, in the end, your own. Before you were born, you, like everyone who was about to be born, were confronted with various choices. Your choice was power. I am that power, and I will stay with you to the end of your days."

"Thanks a lot, mate. There seems to be nothing more to say." Adolph kicked the door open into the doss

house, and then with another almighty kick, slammed it shut again.

"I will teach all those bastards with their... do-gooders... and their stupid lousy coats and boots. He threw the coat on the floor and spat on it. Then unlaced the boots and threw them across the room.

"Mind what you are doing, you crazy sod." A young man, who sat reading, got up from his chair. "You nearly hit me with those boots."

"So what, you lousy git? What difference would a few more bruises make to you? Your arms are full of them already."

"That is none of your bloody business, mate. But what's up with you? You behave like a madman."

"You will find out, when the time is right. In the meantime, just damn well leave me alone." He went over to his bunk bed and threw himself down. Putting his hands behind his head, he then closed his eyes, and started to plan how he was going to see the young Jewish girl again.

Suddenly, Adolph jumped up again. "Come back out here again, mate, I want another word with you!" he shouted.

"What is it now?" Again the stranger spoke from within.

"I have had a thought. Supposing we wait with all that power business until I have seen that girl again?"

"I don't understand?"

"There is nothing for you to understand. All I want is to wait a bit before I take up the power you are talking about. I want to see if it is possible for me to be with someone who truly cares and loves me, and if so, I am prepared to give everything else up for her."

"God help us! Are you planning to fall in love?"

"Why not? The girl is beautiful."

"Beautiful she might be, but so what?"

"I'd like to give it a try. I have never had anyone who truly loved me; perhaps I would have no need of power if I had that."

"All right." The stranger sighed. "I will make a pact with you. If you find you are able to live a happy life with the girl, then I will give you back your soul. Even guide you to make an honest living without stealing paintings." He laughed softly.

"That is all I can ask for. Should it not work out, then I will follow your guidance."

Adolph lay down again. A strange stillness came over him. Would it be possible to love, and have someone to love him, too? Tomorrow would tell.

"Listen, you odd ball." It was the man with the book again. "I don't know what you are on, but for sure, it's something powerful, the way you go on, shouting to yourself. Do you think you could button up and let us have some sleep?"

"Ah! Piss off!" Adolph turned his head to the wall and went to sleep.

Here, the writing had been scratched out. Then, with different ink, Sarah continued her story:

I was not going to write any more; my shame is too great, but having started, it does ease my heart.

Everything I have written so far is the truth. Adolph, my darling Adolph, told me everything. The way he had felt at first towards our race... towards me. His honesty endeared me even more to him.

The reason for his hostility, I will document later on.

He told me how he had made a pact with himself. That if for some terrible reason, our love — for love it was, sweet tender love — was destroyed, and we were separated, then he would annihilate with a mighty power, everything that stood in his way. He frightened me with those words. There was something so intense about the way he spoke, that I believed he would be capable of it.

Adolph and I saw each other regularly, usually in a derelict house on the outskirts of town. I think my poor mother was beginning to wonder why suddenly I had so much shopping to do, and always wanted to go alone.

It is two and a half months since we met, and Christmas is but a week away. Through the frosted glass doors into the dining room, the Christmas tree stands glittering, showing off its lights and fine decorations.

I sat in my room crying, holding my head in my hands, but I had to pull myself together before going down. As I began to pin my unruly hair in place, I could hear the voice of my father downstairs, shouting unusually loudly. He was speaking to Olga, my mother's maid.

"I don't care if you are ten weeks gone... you will have to go." He raised his voice again. "It is a disgrace, having you in our house in that condition. I want you gone by tomorrow morning. There is no more to be said." Then the door slammed.

Olga walked sobbing down the stairs and into the dining room where my mother was busy arranging a few last-minute trinkets under the tree. My mother looked at Olga's tear-stained face, then went to sit down in her high-backed armchair and began stitching a piece of tapestry demurely.

"Olga? Come here, girl!'

Olga walked over to her mistress and stood silently in front of her, with her head bent, trying to dry her eyes with the corner of her apron.

"I am so sorry for what has happened. Come, sit down." My mother pulled a chair out for her. "Sit down, my dear." She took Olga's hand. "I shall miss you, especially now, so close to Christmas. But we don't seem to have any choice. Where will you go, my dear?"

"I have no family, madam." Olga started to cry again. "So I suppose it is the workhouse for me."

"Oh, no, child! You can't mean that. THAT I really cannot allow to happen to one of our staff." My mother spoke with a determined voice, emphasizing the word "that" as only she could.

"I think I have a solution for you. I have an elderly aunt living by herself, in a house much too large for her, in Berlin. I will telephone her and tell her about your situation. I feel sure she will take you in. You will be a comfort to her in her old age, and a great help, as she finds it difficult to get around any more. When the child is born, if you keep it well away from her so that it doesn't disturb her, I am sure you will have no problems."

"I thank you, madam." Olga kissed my mother's hand. "There never was a kinder woman in the whole world than you, madam. And when this is born," she patted her stomach, "I shall name her after you, if it is a girl."

My mother got up from her chair, went over to the Christmas tree, and unhooked one of the beautiful, hand-made glass balls, offering it to her. "Here, my dear, take this. Fragile as it is, it needs looking after carefully, just like you and your unborn child."

Olga took the glass ball, which sparkled in the candlelight.

"Let this be a symbol between us," my mother continued, "that this fragile bauble might be a reminder to us both that all aspects of life need to be respected and loved."

When Christmas had come and gone, our house was strangely quiet, and although no one verbally referred to Olga, we all knew that she was on our minds.

Rabbi Elijah had arrived earlier to wish us a Happy New Year.

I excused myself, and then ran to my room where I was violently sick.

Later, my father called me to come down again. The rabbi was about to leave. He asked me kindly if I was feeling better, unaware that it was not the food that had upset my stomach, but my unborn child!

I kissed him. "Just something that disagreed with me, Papa."

My father... my dear old father, looked at me over his half-moon glasses with his wise old eyes, then touched my cheeks gently.

"You know, kirsling, if there is something you want to talk to me about, I will always be there for you."

"I know, Papa. I love you." I quickly turned my face, so that he should not see how ashamed I felt by deceiving him.

Adolph and I had arranged to meet the following morning. Again, I was to pretend to go to the shops at about the time he was finished cleaning outside our house. He would then follow me to the derelict house, our place of love, and there we would share the food and wine I had taken from our kitchen, before making love on my father's old winter coat.

My darling, darling Adolph; how we loved each other, as we promised to be faithful and true to each other.

On this fatal day, he urged me to run away from home, taking with me only my jewels and whatever money I could lay my hands on. With the proceeds, we hoped to be able to make our way into Germany, where he would try to get into the army, and I could set up home for the three of us. How my heart beat with happiness, just thinking of being with him every day. I was crazy in love, but that did not excuse what I subsequently did...

We both knew that it would be hopeless to tell my parents of our relationship. I had witnessed only a few weeks back what Papa did to Olga. I could not even begin to think what it would do to my poor mother's nerves.

But in the arms of my lover, I put all those thoughts behind me and tried to think only of the moment and its pleasures.

On this day, having eaten our food, Adolph opened up to me for the first time about his background. He told me that his father had Jewish blood in him; his grandfather had been the illegitimate son of a rich Jewish merchant.

"That makes us a quarter the same." He laughed. "So there should not really be any reason for your parents to object to me."

I knew that they never would accept him, so that left only one option... to elope with him.

"My father," he continued sadly, "was a bastard in the true sense of the word. He used to beat and sexually

abuse me, often in front of my mother, who did have some compassion for me, but was unable to do anything but watch helplessly as I lay screaming and bleeding on the floor. Once she did try to stop him, and she ended up with a broken jaw and black eye. Sometimes it was the other way around. I would be forced to watch him doing the same to my mother. I can't say which was the worst."

At that moment I knew, when I saw tears running down his thin, starved face, his black eyes like two deep wells filled with pain, that I would do anything for him. Anything.

I held his dear head in my hands, and then kissed away his tears, as he whispered, "I never had a bloody chance; a damaged childhood, class teachers who would not understand or have patience with me. The one thing I loved and excelled in was art, something I knew I could have made a success of, if only they had accepted me at the academy. But even that, they tore to pieces."

"Very nice." Adolph raised his voice, mimicking his teacher. "Very nice, boy, but can't you paint some figures in those landscapes?"

"No, I bloody couldn't, for if I had, they would have turned out like my father, a monster. But how could I tell them that? So I said nothing, and that was the end of my art. Then I thought, join the army, fight for your country. Oh, I would have done anything to do that. Do

you know what the sergeant told me, when I went to enlist?"

I shook my head, afraid my words might make him stop speaking.

"They laughed at me, and then told me I was not even strong enough to lift a gun. Everyone, everywhere, turned against me after both my parents had died. The council kicked me out on the street and repossessed our home. Now I have nowhere to live, except in the doss house amongst filthy druggies and drunks, and the only job I can get is to shovel snow. Not much of a prospect, is it? But I promise you, I will make good. I will get into the army, and I will show all the bastards who do not believe in me, just what I am capable of."

"Adolph! Adolph, don't say that, you frighten me."

"You know, Sarah, I honestly think you are the only good thing that has happened in my life. When I am with you, I feel a love I have never experienced before, and that frightens me, for I had no intention of falling in love with you. My motives were for a different reason, which is not important now. All that matters to me now is to be with you."

Adolph was only eighteen years old, a year older than I, and had just lost his mother to cancer. I could not bring more unhappiness to him; I had to do as he asked me.

We set a date for two weeks ahead, when I knew my parents would both be away for a week in Germany.

Most of the staff would be given time off. Only Helga, my old nanny, would be at home, seeing to my needs.

Two weeks later, I met Adolph as planned, carrying with me my own and my mother's jewels as well as money I had taken from my father's safe. I was shaking and crying bitterly, not to mention feeling sick, for I was now in the third month of my pregnancy.

Adolph tried to calm me, by whispering loving words in my ears.

We then left to find rooms in a small boarding house at the other end of the town, and there we spent our first night together. I laughed when Adolph said, we were now a proper family, in a room... and with a bed.

"My little wife, I love you and you, too, son," he prodded my expanding belly with a finger. "Together, we will conquer the world!'

"Yes, sir! Sergeant!" I gave a mock salute then jumped out of bed and ran to throw up in the sink.

Suddenly there was a hammering on the door and it burst open.

There stood my father, together with two police officers, staring at us. I tried to cover my nakedness with a towel, whilst Adolph pulled the sheets over him. I will not describe what happened next, only to say that Adolph was dragged off, half-naked, to prison and beaten senseless by the police. I could hear his screams as they threw him into their van.

My father called me a slut and a thief, and refused to listen to me, as he brought me back to the house where my mother lay in a state of nervous collapse.

On their unexpected return, due to some minor problems at my father's bank, they found that my mother's jewels were gone and his safe raided. The police were called, and it didn't take them long to work out what had happened. To find us was not difficult, either, as we were still in the town.

I was locked in my room and guarded every moment of the day and night, until the birth of my beautiful baby boy, whom I called Harry. Harry was taken away from me at three months and sent to England, together with Helga, my nanny, to be brought up by a distant, childless cousin, who had married an English teacher.

As for me, I was sent to the Convent of the Holy Mary, for, as my family told me, I was no longer a daughter of theirs, nor a daughter of their religion.

The kind nuns took me in, and I learned to pray in a different tongue with different words to the same God, who, I was sure, with his goodness and love, would understand.

We have an English gardener at the convent. I have entrusted these documents to him. He has promised to deliver them to my beloved Harry on his next leave. My son will then be twenty years old... a man. He has the right to know about his background, his parents. I heard from the gardener how Adolph, after our separation, developed such a hatred for the Jews that he swore he would exterminate them all. I pray to God that he will find peace in his heart, though the news I get from trusted friends is heartbreaking.

Here the document finished abruptly.

Chapter 16

Grace put the papers down in total shock, not wanting to accept the truth of what she had been reading. Was this girl telling her that she was the mother of her father and that Adolph Hitler was his father? But that meant that Hitler was also her grandfather…

It couldn't be! Her sweet, loving father couldn't have had Hitler as his father. That monster! That madman, who was responsible for the extermination of millions. No, it must be someone else with the same name she was referring to. Oh, dear God, let it be someone else with the same name.

She would have to ask her mother if she knew anything about it.

With shaking hands, she put the papers back in the folder and then, with an uneasy mind, went to bed. Grace couldn't sleep; tossing and turning, her senses were spinning with what she had read. What was she to do? Should she show them to her mother — for she was sure her mother had no knowledge of them — or burn them?

Thoughts came to her that there was no kindness in destroying people's illusions. She got out of bed and put the light on, took the papers out of the folder and fed them one by one into the flames of the open fire, but not before making a note of the convent where Sarah was taken to in Vienna.

One day, she thought, *I will find out the truth from her, if she is still alive.* But how was she to keep it from her mother, who had become very fragile, never really recovering from the death of her husband?

Grace put the light out again and tried to sleep.

She began dreaming. She dreamed she was lying in her bed looking out of the window at the star-filled sky. She wondered about Night. Did it like being out there, shutting the light out from everyone's life? She thought to herself, *I will go and ask it a few questions...*

After getting up from her bed, she put on her heavy coat and thought, *Now, where is the best place to go and have a chat*, for as she looked around, it seemed to her that Night was everywhere at the same time. Where was his head, and where was his tail?

She stood for a long time, just looking at the sky, where the windows to the feast in Heaven were open. She could clearly see the movements of the guests as they danced in front of the brightly lit windows.

Thank God Night cannot be there to send out his dark vapours among those dancing guests, she thought. *Someone must be there standing guard, otherwise, he would surely try to be there, too.*

A cold hand slapped her across the face. She spun around. "What did you do that for?" she asked the ugly face of Darkness. "When all I did was come out here to ask you a few questions?"

"I always slap the face of anyone wanting to know me," he said. "For how else would you know that I am here?"

"Pardon me, we obviously have different customs. Here, we need only to shake hands to be introduced," Grace replied.

"But how would you know with whom you are shaking hands if you shake hands with everyone you meet?" Darkness said, peering at her with small dark eyes, black as coal in an even darker face.

"What is it you want to know?" Darkness continued. "I have little time to spend with you... you and I obviously don't understand each other and should therefore try to avoid meeting at all costs. But since we are here together, walk with me and I will show you what my duties are. Then if you want to know anything else, I may or may not be able to tell you."

"Wait a moment," she urged. "Let me light a candle to take with me, so that I will be able to see where we are going, and find my way back home again." She lit the candle she held in her hand.

Night shrank back. "Don't you ever do that when you are with me," he shouted, throwing his cloak around the flame. "Don't you know that by lighting a candle you eliminate my powers, and I will not be able to see?" He raised his cloak and blew out the candle. So now

Grace had no choice but to take his hand and follow him, for she certainly could not see where to go.

"No need to hold back," he said, as he pulled her along. "I will see you safely back."

Unsure about this adventure, she looked towards the castle in the sky where millions of lights still shone from its festive windows. *I will always have their light,* she thought. "Let us go," she said bravely.

They walked for some time in silence. Then she asked Night, "Do you like to always be in darkness?"

"Darkness? What do you mean?" Night answered back. "In my world, I can see perfectly well, it is only with your eyes, everything seems invisible."

"Don't you ever want to come out and see the other side of life?" she asked. "That of light?"

"Everyday, I see that other side of life, as you call it, and I can only say that I have no wish to be part of that, or anything at all to do with it. I see how people with open eyes stumble more in that light than they do in mine, and I will not be responsible for their injuries or their blindness."

"Do you always travel at this speed?" Grace asked breathlessly. For it seemed as if they were travelling faster and faster though she could not see the road they were leaving behind, nor that in front of them.

"We have a lot of ground to cover." Night fastened his wings and told her to hold tight to his hand. "Speed is essential." He ascended into the cool night air. "Already the Sun god in the east has begun to stir in her sleep, and once she is awake, there will be no holding her." He pulled her hand harder. "Come along. It was you who wished for my company."

They entered a house where all was in darkness except for one corner where an old man sat leaning over an untidy table, reading an old, worn book.

"See him?" said Darkness. "I had been a friend of his for years until one day when he found that book." Darkness pointed to the heavy book with its gilded pages, the first of which read Bible. Its pages were slowly being turned by hands crippled with age.

"When he found that book, he had no more use for me. Now he shuts me out with that infernal light burning in front of him all night. I can't understand what he finds so interesting in that book. We used to spend nights crying and drinking together, going over and over the battlefields of his life. He was always awake when I came and always greeted me as an old friend. Now he locks me out… does not even see me. Last night I even found him smiling as he went to sleep. I don't know what my world has come to."

Grace pointed to the candle glowing on the table. "Perhaps it is that tiny flame from his candle which has bewitched him. See how attentively and lovingly he guards it with his old hands."

"That tiny light should know better," said Darkness, "than to try to take over my territories. Come, let us leave. I can see that he is not going to notice me at all." Darkness pointed towards the bent figure.

"Anyway, he will soon come back to me when the flame burns out. Until that day, let him amuse himself. I have others I must not neglect."

They had not gone far before they silently crept into a room high up beneath the eaves. At first Grace did not think anyone could live in such a place. Bottles and discarded food boxes were strewn all around.

"Here, truly, is a friend of mine," said Darkness. "You will see how welcome I am here." He approached the sleeping figure on the bed and shook him awake.

"Darkness, my old friend!" exclaimed the toothless figure, stretching his arms towards them. "How I long for you to take me in your arms forever, never having to face the confounded light again, for it never ceases to point out to me my surroundings, whereas you let me be and help me not to see. Come, let us have a game of hide-and-seek. Tell me, Darkness, who am I?"

Darkness again shook the toothless man and told him that it was of no importance who he was, for in darkness, all were alike, and nothing was asked of anyone there, except to be part of it.

"That foolish man," Darkness whispered to Grace, "can't he see that what he is matters little to me and the likes of me? But we must all pretend to keep his spirits up."

Darkness turned and faced the old man. "Keep awake, friend, and I will stay with you until the sun comes out, so that you will not be alone." And with that,

Darkness walked out, but left his shadows behind to cover the old man.

Grace was horrified. "Why do you encourage such an existence?"

Darkness looked at her. "If you want to be part of me, this is what I have to offer. You can always leave if you are bored."

It seemed to Grace that all she had seen so far was human misery. Surely there would be something else to learn about Darkness. "Do you ever feel lonely?" she asked.

"Lonely? What is that word? I have never heard of it. How can you be lonely if you are complete? I have heard Light telling me that within her domain, there are many people living who have an abundance of everything, but still have this feeling you call loneliness. I can only put it down to the fact that these people see so many things they want and perhaps long for them if they cannot have them. Where I rule, none of these things are shown. So the wants are not there."

Darkness stopped outside a mansion. "Here you will see something exceptional, for here lives a man who has everything in his life, yet he cannot be without me, for his very existence is built of my material." He spun around so as to show his cloak in its full splendour. "From an outsider's point of view, this person is a normal happy being, but I know his soul… his soul joined my cloak a long time ago. I remember clearly when it was, for it was at a time when I had first started this route. The wind was bitterly cold, and I had put on my best winter cloak. I heard a cry, which rose up into the tall rooftops you see over there." He pointed with his bony hands towards the distance.

"I had just finished holding the hand of a young girl walking through the churchyard and was on my way back when I heard it, and went to investigate. I found my friend here, lamenting, asking me to take him under my cloak, for he could not live with himself any longer. You see, this is what he told me: a long time ago he committed a deed, which even to this day he is not able to share with me. However much he tried to be a righteous, loving human being, that deed lay within him as a poison, and he could find no relief in anything he had done since that day.

"I have kept him warm with my cloak, stirred the gloomy weather blowing within it for him, for what use is my good cloak if there is nothing for it to keep warm? As the storm blows, I gather the logs of all the miseries in the world to throw on his fire, to make sure that he will always be part of me."

"But how does he live?" Grace asked. "How does he enjoy life's beautiful moments?"

"He does not, for as soon as he even tries to enjoy himself, I just have to blow on the ashes I have left behind, and they will immediately cloud everything else over. He dared not be happy for fear of me leaving him, for I am the only one who truly understands him."

"I feel sorry for you and for him," she said. "I hope that I shall never be dependent on you. I am sorry to say that, and I don't mean to offend you, but your world is not one which I would like to be part of."

Darkness grinned at her. "You are part of me or else you would not be here. Did you think it was just curiosity that drove you out into this darkness? No, my friend, it was to learn something about yourself, to which only I can give you the answer. So tell me, what is it you really want?"

"Darkness," she whispered, "I only want to know one thing. Why do you move into people's hearts and take their souls? What business is it of yours? Why can't you stay away? Why do you have to destroy what people have taken many years to build, and why do you not care what people are feeling? Don't you know about feelings?"

"I thought you only wanted to know one thing, but since you want to know so much, let us sit down, because my night has been long, and I am beginning to get tired." Darkness spread his cloak, and they both sat down.

"As to your first question: why do I move into people's hearts? Let me tell you. I don't go anywhere unless I am invited in, and I only stay as long as people can bear to have me there, for I can be a heavy fellow to carry around.

"As for taking their souls, I don't know what you are talking about. When I am invited in, I must have something to live on. It seems to me that the thing for which those people have the least use for, is what you call a soul, so naturally, that is what I take, and once it is taken, I can tell you that people will have a job getting it back from me again.

"And as for destroying… again, I don't know what you are talking about. I don't see that I am destroying anything. On the contrary, I give life to that other side of man, which otherwise would not be known and, as I said, I can only do that if I am invited to do so. So it seems to me that I am doing a favour to the ones who cannot live without me and whom I never destroy. When I move in, the destruction has already taken place, otherwise, how would I live there?"

Darkness continued, "I cannot live in a house where light may possibly be seen. No, I have to live in a house that has been destroyed, so that light cannot penetrate and disturb me. Clearly, my friend, we do not see life the same way, therefore, our togetherness will have to end, for with you, I would never have any rest or peace. But before I leave you, a word of warning. When you next go in search of answers to your questions, get your facts right before wasting the time of whoever it is you may trouble."

As the sun sent its rosy red kiss up over the hilltop, Darkness gathered his cloak about him and went on his way. Grace tried to see what was his head and what was his tail, but still could not make it out.

"Goodnight!" he shouted, then tore his wings off before fading into the light.

As Darkness left, Grace sat down on a dew-covered stone. She was totally exhausted. "Why on Earth did I spend all night with that dark fellow?" she asked herself. But before she could answer herself, she felt the soft touch of Day on her face, stretching her long, manicured fingers, touching everything, waking everything up.

"You are up early!" She glittered with sunlight. "What kept you awake?"

"Night," Grace told her with a groan.

"Oh, that old misery. What has he been up to now?" Sun touched her brow.

Grace told her about her adventure with Night.

"Never confuse Night with Darkness, for they are not the same." Sun smiled. "Darkness is the unruly cousin of Night and should never be confused with him. I see that it was Darkness who took you in hand last night, for Night himself would have been far too busy to take you on such a journey. Besides, when he enters, it is always with joy, for he is nature's sleeping powder in order that all may have a rest from me." As she said this, she broke into merry laughter.

"I am so full of adventures that however much I would like to be part of everyone the whole time, people do tire of me and want to rest. Then they will look forward to seeing me again. Darkness, the old misery, is always trying to gather more gloomy thoughts around him. He needs them for his protection, otherwise, he would not be strong enough to survive. As a rule, Night leaves him alone, but sometimes Sleep will send him packing. A fight can even take place.

"I saw this one day, when a small child who had cried for her mother for a month was calling for Sleep. Darkness saw his chance and stood in the corner waiting for Sleep to give up his work. Fortunately, Sleep saw him there and chased him out. Darkness hit back with a gust of ice-cold wind, which made the little girl shiver and pull her blankets up over her ears. Sleep then started to rock her in his arms, and the little girl slept as she had never slept before. I was there myself to kiss her good morning when it was time for her to wake."

She looked at Grace's weary face. "It seems you could do with some sleep yourself. I don't know if Sleep is working overtime, but if you go home, I will try to find him and send him to you. Goodnight, dear friend."

"Goodnight, beautiful Day," Grace replied, "and thank you."

Sleep did come, though she was not sure who of them slept first. Grace awoke as Light was getting ready for her departure to the other side of the mountain. Grace did not see her again, for she herself was to travel over many mountains and every time she thought she had caught up with her, she was just disappearing behind yet another mountain.

Day made many friends on her journey, but most of them she would rather forget, for they left nothing with her other than some of their own rubbish, no longer wanted and too heavy for them to carry.

"But there are always a few who will stay in my heart," she said, "and whenever I think about them, I seem to grow in wealth. Being alone does not seem such a terrible thing, for as I am part of all that is of life, then that must also be part of me. So Loneliness, though at times she shows her empty basket and asks for bread and eggs, does not often call on me. She knows from long standing that although I will fill her basket, the fare she gets from me, she could do as well without.

"Loneliness is a strange creature. Let me tell you about her. She is a she... that I am sure of. Not by her face or her dress, but by that sudden entry she makes into my life, almost as an apology. Then, once in, she suddenly changes and becomes bold.

"'Why not?' she will shout. 'Why not come with me?' Then she shows me her true character. She cries, she begs, she flings her naked arms around me, until I can no longer withstand her and go with her. Two more lonely beings you will never see, for Loneliness does not want anyone to touch her or be near her. She likes to suffer alone, and though she allows me to travel with her, I am never completely part of her."

"Is it always lonely where you go?" Grace asked, trying to take it all in. Then she remembered the advice of Darkness. *My God! What a stupid question,* she thought, and shut up. Loneliness was so immersed in herself and her misery that she did not even hear her. Just as well.

What on Earth do I talk to her about? Grace wondered. *I can't think of one single thing.*

But Loneliness obviously did not feel the same for she asked her, "In your world where you have so many choices, why do you follow me?"

"Perhaps because we have all those choices," Grace replied. "We get confused about what to have and be part of, and in the end, we end up with nothing."

"Seems a strange world to me." Loneliness looked sadly at her. "At least in my world there is only the one thing. I never get confused."

"Do you always travel alone, or with people like me who are confused?" Grace asked.

"No, many times I have the companionship of Bitterness. He is a terrible fellow... I can smell him from here. Stay away from him if you can." Her voice shook. "He would make you very bitter if you bit into him.

"Then there is Unhappiness. He is a crooked fellow, for he always makes people see the wrong things and he is so bent over with the heavy burdens they place on him, that he can no longer straighten his back. But he likes to keep me company when he has nothing else to do, for we speak the same dialect, and he was brought up in the same town. He often laughs when he tells his stories of how he can make the most sensible man believe him, when no one else will listen to them any more. I tell you, he is very crooked, so listen carefully to what he says to you, for he will always try to make you see the worst side. Still, he is very old and must be excused for some of his mischief.

"Then there is Hate. Now I will not travel with Hate, for she always brings out her instruments to show me. With these instruments, she will prod people so that they can no longer stand her, then they will act out her evil ploy. She is evil, to say the least, and I feel sorry for the people who use her instruments, for they are always the ones who are hurt first.

"Then, sometimes, I have my old friend, professor of all knowledge. Now he is interesting. Whatever I ask him about, he always has an intelligent answer. I sometimes amuse myself by trying to ask him something which I think he does not know the answer to. I have never yet succeeded. I think that I could almost love him," said Loneliness, with a slight blush on her pale face. "But of course, he is so busy with his worldly interests that he never would consider such a one as me. Anyway, were I to go with him, I suppose I would endanger my very species."

"You seem to have a very interesting life and many who keep you company. Perhaps I should not trouble you any more." Grace got up to leave. "I, too, must go and be part of my life, but I wish you well on your journey, and I will try to remember your warnings."

Grace turned in her sleep.

Early the next morning, when Grace woke up, the sun was just rising. Birds were singing outside her window, and the pink cherry blossom blew about in the gentle breeze.

Good God, what a strange dream! She got up, rubbing her eyes. *What is happening to me? I don't seem to be able to follow my own thoughts any more. Perhaps some madness has taken hold of me?*

Stop it, silly… she stuck her tongue out at herself as she looked in the mirror above her bed. *It was only a dream for Christ's sake. I had better get some fresh air to clear my head.* She jumped out of bed, then pulled on a warm grey jumper, a heavy, warm skirt and stout walking shoes before walking quickly out into the dew-soaked university grounds, then continued through the black iron gates out to the rocky moorland stretching for miles through the landscape.

Not a soul was around, except for a few herons standing on one leg as still as statues, waiting to catch one thing or another. *They are just like me,* she thought ironically. *Perhaps, if I stand still on one leg and focus my mind, I might be able to catch the truth about my life.*

She bent one leg under her, and then tried to stand still. The herons looked at her almost mockingly when she nearly fell over, as the ground was soft from last night's rain.

Dear God! What am I to do? In her mind she tried to make sense of the letter Sarah had written.

She sat down on a boulder and started to write.

Oh, life! What is it you gave me? A stone to sit on when, weary and tired, my feet cannot walk any more? The cold comfort of a morning damp with tears from yesterday? Did you awaken me to sample the mist as it gathers the blanket, which only the rays of the sun can penetrate? I wake up, but find as I am sitting here, that though life bids me "Good Morning" and though I am awaiting the joy of the day, I cannot remember having walked this road before, though it seems to me that nothing is new.

Can it be that we all awaken anew with the sweetness of the before, as part of one's tears, as part of one's laughter?

I am not so sure. But what is it then, which awakens these stumbling thoughts, these lights of memories within? Could it be that as I look at the sky together with the birds flying above me, that both of us wake up in the same instant, both of us realise in that same instant, the glory of a new day?

No darkness can penetrate the sweet memory of yesterday, its pleasures, its new awakenings, its pain, and its disappointments. But as life takes my hand and bids me follow it through its narrow passage, through its wide roads, I see no other choice but to follow.

For should it not be so that that which has been of life — for a lifetime before me — must know where to go? For as I came into this world, stumbling, unsure, knowing not whether to take the one road or the other, it would be safe to take the hand of life when offered, it would be wise to sample the food she has prepared for me.

For should I think that I could cook and bake an equal fare, then life would gently tell me, "You have a lot to learn." For have I not been here before your father's forefathers? Was I not the one who drank of their joy, their sorrow? Was I not the one who woke them to the bitter news and, equally, to their sweetness? I do not hurry or tarry. But I move with each breath, each movement of you.

I do not complain of the tiredness, which touches me when the day is finished. Nor do I regret the time we spend together, for as one enters my life, so the other must be finished. I do, many times, uphold my duties, though the child in my hands struggles and cries, "Let me go," and the windows of darkness are shut to the light.

I try... I honestly try, to make you go hither, to sample the crop which lies on the other side. For as each day must be ready to greet the light, so it must be prepared when the darkness descends. For in knowing the equal length of both, we must realise that nothing can ever be of just the one.

"Rejoice, child, in the morning as it spreads its glorious wings over a desert, bare of love and fruitfulness. Rejoice of the evening, as he, dark and powerful, draws the darkness in by turning the clock."

I cannot begin to remember when last we met, but still the memory of that day, that moment, is part of me again. For as the sun sends its rays to touch and caress, so I must, without knowing, be part of that which it touched before. For is one not constant to the other? Is the one not equal to that which was sent yesterday? Was it not from the same source?

Oh, good child, who follows me, who touches on me, rejoice that our togetherness can leave joyful moments in the hearts of all who taste this flavour. All who wake to the sound of the cry, who hear the laughter as it travels up towards the light and penetrates the smallest crevice.

Oh, my God in Heaven, do I retreat my footsteps to the narrow path spreading in front of me? Or do I try the river with its leaking boat? Or, perhaps, the steep mountain track as it twists and turns in its wake? Do I bend with the sorrow, or do I lift off its cover? Do I silently listen without comment, though the wisdom is missing in the portion served? Do I sit and let harmony be destroyed by the anger, the frustration of a mind, which can only see the shallowness of self?

Where do I step in — if at all? Or do I just as now, retreat, let be, until another day, another moment? If so, do I honestly allow myself to sample this foul wine, or do I spit it out? Do I just sit here, without even trying to wash out the narrow ear, without even trying to make the eye see? I know in my heart that two things have happened, as the tide washed ashore the empty can of worms.

Enough… Grace got up from where she was sitting. "Dad?" she called softly. "Dad, if you can hear me, wherever you are, help me to clear my mind, for I am totally lost." She wiped away a tear with her fingertips, then put her pen and papers down.

"Oh, Dad, how I wish that for just one moment you could return and give me some advice. I feel so helpless and alone; I don't seem to be able to speak with Mum any more. She locked herself within a shell after you died, and it is difficult for me to speak with my friends. It is all so depressing. I don't want to make them unhappy on my behalf." Tears ran down her face.

Suddenly, the image of her father walked slowly towards her. He was wearing his old brown ink-stained jacket, and holding his beloved pipe in his hand.

"Child! Though I left you, I am always with you." His voice was like the soft whisper of the wind. "Why do you weep over me?"

Grace felt faint with shock, then grabbed hold of the side of the boulder and held on for dear life. She tried to speak, but no sound came out.

"Dad… Dad!" she managed to whisper. "Is it really you?"

Her father took her hand. "It is the image of me. Like a mirage in the desert, transported here by energy from the atmospheric pressures. As soon as they change, you will not see me any more. The level of consciousness I find myself on is high above this one. On that consciousness, no body is needed, as you yourself will discover when we meet there again."

"Is it far from here, Dad?" she whispered, unable to believe her eyes and ears.

"Yes, Grace, it has taken me this long, what is it… seven years now, to come back just this once."

"Dad, I found your letters from Sarah. Tell me it isn't true about you being *that* Hitler's son. I couldn't live with that knowledge. That evil monster, my grandfather, hereditarily part of me."

"Child, we do not choose our parents, that is one of the mysteries of birth. What happened, happened. Two people, however wrong for each other, fell in love and out of that love was born another. We are not to judge their actions, nor condemn them for the consequence. Let God be the judge to deal with that in due course. Don't cry, Grace. Do you love me less by knowing from whose loins I sprang? I don't think so.

"Your grandmother is a pious woman. I had the opportunity to visit her once in the convent in Vienna, long before I was married to your mother. My adopted family phoned and told me about the journal — also where they would hide it, should anything happen to them. Remember, it was wartime.

"You would love your grandmother. She is an exceptional woman, living in stillness and peace at the Convent of Santa Maria in Vienna, and perhaps the only person alive today who knows that behind that twisted, distorted mind of your grandfather, there once lived a man who was capable of feelings and love for another, for I was born out of that love. Love between two young people, unaware of the devastating effect their action was to have on humanity and the world today. For a short time, they were just two young people in love. Never forget that."

The image of her father started to fade.

"Dad! Da-a-a-d, don't leave yet! I need to know... do I tell Mum about the papers, or does she already know?"

"No, child; she does not. That was my secret. There was a time just after Jane died that I almost told her. You were the reason for that."

"I remember, Dad. I told you that I had met the Führer on my way down to Earth."

"So you did, and I can tell you it gave me a shock... you did right in burning the papers. I should have done so years ago but somehow did not have the courage to sever the link to my parents.

"Child, I am free of all Earthly dilemmas. I only wish that I could make your mind as peaceful. But you, child, have to find your own peace, which lies together with great wisdom deep within your soul. So continue with your writing, as we both were destined to do. That is our gift. We chose the same gift when confronted with different options.

"Go and visit your grandmother. Give her your blessings before she dies, for I feel your heart closing to her. Open it, child; see the beauty in her soul. You will like her, but don't tell her about this meeting, only that I love her and am happily waiting to be together with her again and that always, deep in my heart, I loved her.

"A mother's love will reach her child, however great the distance. And to your mother, just kiss her from me. Again, don't tell her about our meeting, for in her delicate state, she would not be able to cope with it.

"Grace, many years into the future, there will be something called Thought Travel on Earth, and the way you and I speak now, will be the norm. But for now, it can only happen very rarely, and even when it does, few people on Earth have the ability to perceive what they hear and see.

"I will try to come back again in the future, as I have done today, but in the meantime, I will help you to speed up your gift of writing. Helping your teachers within. Oh yes! Don't look so surprised, I know all about them, but you realise of course, that your teachers are only a mental vision from your subliminal mind."

Grace nodded. "I know, Daddy, but it is very much like a classroom in a school."

"Indeed, child, for recollecting takes a lot of energy and mind powers to be sorted out and made sense of, having lain buried there for so long." Her father smiled. "I will send you words of wisdom that I have learned on the higher level of consciousness. Oh yes! There are classes there on Life, wherever it is; a never-ending process of learning, but learning such as cannot be imagined on Earth. Perhaps mankind will be ready for that in time. I will be, in a sense, your spiritual teacher, since I am no longer of the Earth. I will help you to formulate and correct your work." He smiled again. "That will be my gift to you."

With that, her father faded, and Grace was left sitting on the cold rock, wondering if, once again, she had dreamt it all. Then she suddenly saw her father's pipe lying in the grass. She ran to pick it up. It was still warm and alight.

"Oh, Daddy, Daddy!" Grace threw herself down on the wet grass, crying her eyes out. Then suddenly she heard her father's voice again, as strong as if he were standing next to her.

"Get up, child. I did not come to make you unhappy. I came to bring you my gift of beauty and wisdom from beyond. Treasure them well."

"I will, Dad."

Grace stood up and tried to rub some of the wet mud off her shoes and skirt. But in the end, she gave up and quickly walked, still holding her father's pipe, back towards the black iron gates and up the drive that would take her to the university and her studies.

Chapter 17

A blue post van followed Grace through the gates. The postman rolled down his window then, smiling, greeted her. "Good morning, miss. You are an early riser." Collins, the old postman, loved by all the university students for his cheery ways, was about to deliver the post. Leaving the van, he slammed the door and then took another look at Grace.

"What has happened to you?" He peered with concern at her dirty skirt and shoes. "Did you fall over?"

She smiled. "Something like that, Collins, but I picked myself up again."

"Good. I am glad to hear that, miss... and you should stop smoking." He pointed to the pipe in her hand. "Pipes are not for young ladies."

"No, Collins, you are right, they are not. I will never do it again. Do you have any letters for me today?"

"Not today, miss. But I believe there was one yesterday."

"I haven't had it yet. I wonder why it was not brought to my room?"

"I couldn't say, miss, but hopefully it will be good news, if that is what you are waiting for."

"We are all waiting for good news; I hope mine is that I have passed my exams, for I shall be leaving at the end of the summer."

"I am sorry to hear that… I shall miss you."

"And I shall miss you, too, Collins. You are a good sort."

"Thank you, miss. Where will you go when you leave?"

"I will go back to see my mother. She is not well."

"I am sorry to hear that, too. Is it serious?"

"I don't know, but she has not been well for the last seven years since my father died. This is his pipe, by the way."

"It happens like that sometimes. When two people have been very close, the one left behind does not want to carry on alone, and they give up their spirit, but I hope she will soon recover." Collins opened the back of the post van and took out a large bundle of letters.

"I don't think so, Collins. She has lost all interest in life. All she does is sit reading my father's poems all day."

Collins closed the door of his van. "And a mighty fine writer he was, too, miss. I have two of his books at home… even the missus, who never opens a book, reads them. I am very proud to know his daughter!"

"Oh, Collins, don't say that, for I haven't done anything yet. But I like to write, too, and maybe one day I will be able to send you a volume of mine."

"That will be a great day, miss. I shall be looking forward to receiving it. What might you be calling it?"

"I think, *Your Gift*. My father always talked about the gifts we were given at birth, and how we had to recognize and develop them."

"Your father was a wise man, miss. I am sorry I never met him, he was too young to die."

"I know, Collins, there are times when I think life is really cruel. Just look back in history and remember what has taken place. It seems that whatever we build up and begin to enjoy, after some time, always seems to crumble."

"Those are dark words on such a beautiful morning, miss, and not thoughts for a young lady like you. Life will always give you something in return for what it takes."

"Spring and summer take over from winter, and winter from autumn, but each season gives us something of itself worth having. All we have to do is work with it, not against it. Oh, look, I'd better get these letters delivered. It was nice speaking with you, miss."

"Thank you, Collins. I enjoyed it, too."

"Have a good day, miss, and good luck with yesterday's letter. Let me know if you have passed."

"I will, Collins. See you!" She held the door for him as they both entered the university.

Grace ran to her room, where four letters lay on a blue metal plate on her table. "Four letters... where did they come from?" Three of them were without stamps, just bearing her name.

"From us, you silly!" Lisa and Betty, her two bubbly roommates stood grinning in the doorway. "To wish you congratulations. Haven't you seen the noticeboard downstairs? Your name is on it. Open your letter!"

Grace opened the formal grey envelope. It was an invitation to join Oxford University to take a master's degree in English literature.

"I don't want to take it up." Grace laid the letter down. "I am going home to look after my mother, and then I will do some travelling."

Lisa and Betty looked stunned.

"Give it to me, then." Red-haired Lisa snatched it from the table. "I will pretend to be you and take your place, if you don't want it." Jokingly, she danced around with it. "But no such luck," she said sadly as she threw herself on her bed.

"I have to go home, too. There is no more money for my studies, so the most I can hope for with my life is to teach noisy infant classes their ABC. Oh well! There is a place for us all." She got up again. "Come, Betty, let's go down and see what the cook has managed to dish up for us poor students today. Are you coming, Grace?"

"Not yet. I will see you later. Oh… wait!"

They both turned around and looked at her.

"There is no point in me staying on to the end of term. I have already passed my exam, and my mother needs me. She is not well."

"Oh, Grace! We are so sorry. You will keep in touch, won't you?"

"I will, don't worry. I just need time to sort myself out."

Grace gathered her few belongings together, then finished her packing, and without saying goodbye to her tutors, walked out of the university and ran to the bus station, where she caught the bus to London.

Sitting on the bus, she composed a letter of apology to her tutors and, on reaching London, bought a stamp and posted it. Then she called a taxi to take her home.

On arriving home, Grace noticed the overgrown garden and neglected window shutters where most of the paint had peeled away. *We need a gardener to sort this mess out, but can we afford it?* Her mother never mentioned their financial situation. Somehow, she always imagined they had enough but now, looking at the state of the house and garden, she wondered.

Grace rang the front door bell. After three rings, she finally heard slowly approaching footsteps in the hallway. Jane, her mother's old maid, a woman of about sixty-five with a sweet smile on her wrinkled face, opened the door.

"Good gracious. Where did you come from?"

"The bus station. I have finished college." She laughed, giving Jane a hug.

"But, my dear." Jane helped her with her coat. "I didn't know they had broken up already? We didn't expect you before next month."

"They haven't. I have left before the end of term."

Jane gave a loud gasp, holding her hand in front of her mouth. "Whatever happened, Miss Grace?"

"Nothing, Jane. After receiving my exam results today, I decided to come straight home to help you look after Mother."

"What a noble gesture! Did you get the results you wanted?"

"I passed, and have been offered a place at Kings College, Oxford to take my master's in English literature."

"Congratulations… and how pleased Madam will be to see you. She hardly ever moves from her room. Not even to the garden. Perhaps, now that you are back, you can get her to go out a little."

"I will try, Jane, and thank you for looking after her so well. You have been an angel!"

"Not quite, Miss Grace. But on a lovely day like today, we won't talk about that." She winked, giving a wicked grin.

"Well, you have to us; I can never repay you for all your kindness to my mother."

"I have already been paid a hundredfold, miss. No one is kinder than your mother… a true lady, if I may say so. If only you could get her to enjoy life a little."

"I shall do my best. And Jane, I am starving, I haven't eaten since this time last night. Would you be able to make me a cold salad?"

"Certainly, miss. Do you want me to bring it to your mother's room?"

"No, Jane. Prepare a table on the patio for two with a good bottle of wine. Actually, make that three; you come and join us. I will bring Mother down. Let us enjoy this beautiful day."

"That sounds lovely, Miss Grace. I will start to prepare it right away. I have some fine ham and cheese with freshly baked bread."

"I can smell it. Delicious! I will just run up to see Mother."

Grace took the stairs two at a time, then knocked on her mother's door.

"Come in, Jane. You don't have to knock." Anna's voice sounded old and tired.

"It is not Jane, Mother, it is me!"

"Oh! My dearest dear, when did you arrive? Why are you not at university?" Anna was lying prostrate on her chaise longue with a blanket over her, in spite of the intense heat from an open fire. Her auburn hair had turned snow white. With a faraway look in her eyes, she gazed intensely at Grace.

"My dearest." She patted the end of the chaise longue. "Sit down and tell me all about it."

"There is not much to tell. I had my exam results today, with an invitation to go to Oxford for my master's. I just decided to leave early."

"How long are you staying?"

"For good, Mum. I am not going back. I am staying with you."

"But Grace, your studies. What about them?"

"I can do all the studying I want from home. I am not concerned about that."

"Oh! My dear, I am so pleased to see you." Anna squeezed her hand. "I am getting so awfully tired lately. I don't know why…"

"You should see a doctor, Mum!"

"What for? All they do is give you a pill to prolong your agony. I will have nothing of that."

"What do you mean, Mum? Are you really ill?"

"I have been ill for a long time, dear. Leukaemia! I saw a Harley Street specialist some years ago. There is no cure. But I have been determined to fight on until you finished your studies. Now that you are back, I can begin to let go."

"Mama, dear Mama! Why did you not tell me before?" Grace hugged her, as she felt tears welling up in her eyes. "I would have come back sooner."

"I know you would." Anna gave a brief, tired smile. "That's what I didn't want. You have your whole long life in front of you and need your education so that you can take care of yourself when I am gone, which I am sure will not be long now."

"Don't say that, Mum." Tears were streaming down Grace's cheeks. "What am I going to do without you?" she cried.

"Shush, child! No tears, we have had enough of that. Shush! Shush! Here, have this." Anna gave her a chocolate.

Grace shook her head.

"Go ahead. Eat it. You will see it will make you feel better. They are from Fortnum and Mason... can you believe it? They sent me a whole kilo of this lot last week. Poor Jane is sick of eating them. Tells me they are no good for her complexion."

In spite of herself, Grace couldn't help laughing.

"That's my girl! But since we are on more serious subjects, just let me tell you something first. Everything I own I have left to you. The house is fully paid for, and there is money invested in bank shares. Enough to give you a comfortable living. Your father, God bless him, was paid well for the three books he managed to publish before his demise. I have never touched a penny of that; it is all there for you."

"But Mum, how have you been able to live, if not on Daddy's money? You have always been so generous with my allowances. How did you manage that?"

"My dear, I sold the copyright for the cake recipes I used to make for Fortnum and Mason all those years ago. Remember?"

Grace nodded.

"They still make my cakes the traditional way. I make a good living out of that."

"I didn't know, Mum, you never said. Why?"

"Oh! Somehow my achievements were not so important, not worth talking about. However much I enjoyed the money, it gave us a good living."

"You have a great talent for baking, Mum. That is a gift. You should have written a cookery book, it would have been wonderful."

"Perhaps, but all that is in the past." Anna dabbed the perspiration from her face with a delicate lace handkerchief. "I sold the copyright, and that is that."

There was a knock on the door.

"Jane, you don't have to knock." Anna started to laugh softly. "Oh dear, I seem to be repeating myself. Come in, Jane."

"Madam, how wonderful to see you in such good humour. It has done you good to have Grace back."

"Yes, Jane, it has," she replied as she stroked her daughter's hair.

"Madam, there is a cold lunch served on the patio. May I help you down?"

"Do you think I should?" she looked anxiously at her.

"I do, madam." She gently took her arm and helped her up. "Perhaps Miss Grace will take the other arm."

Grace tried not to show how shocked she was to see how thin her mother had become, no more than skin and bones. She put on a bright smile.

"That's right, madam," Jane said encouragingly as Anna took a few slow steps. "Easy does it! It is a wonderful sunny day, the birds are singing in the garden and the trees are all full of blossom."

They slowly walked down the stairs and sat Anna in a comfortable chair on the patio. Jane opened the bottle of red wine then poured a little into Anna's glass, before filling her own and Grace's. She then took off her white apron and straightened her grey dress, before sitting down and raising her glass. "A toast to you, madam, and to you, Miss Grace. Welcome back!"

"Thank you, Jane. I can't tell you how pleased I am to be here. I should not have stayed away so long."

"You are back now, miss; that is all that matters. Now try this ham, it's off the bone and cost an arm and a leg. That is almost funny." She laughed. "I shouldn't say that. The poor pig." She took a mouthful. "Delicious!"

Anna took a few bites. "You are right, Jane, it is delicious. And the bread, I do believe you are using one of my recipes?"

"I am, madam. You always have, the best recipes for bread and cakes."

In spite of everything, Grace found herself eating with great enjoyment. The wine was delicious, too; a full-bodied red wine, as dark as the blueberries growing on the bushes at the end of the garden.

"This is so lovely." Anna gave a contented sigh. "What a wonderful surprise to have you back, Grace. But now I am getting tired. Do you think I could have my coffee in my room, Jane? Then I will have a little sleep."

"Of course, madam."

Both Grace and Jane got up to help Anna back to her room. She looked exhausted. After making her comfortable, Jane went down to fetch the coffee. Grace sat down beside her mother, holding her hand.

"My dearest." Anna opened her eyes and looked at her. "I shall be leaving you soon, I can feel it. I shall go to your father who is waiting for me. Don't be sad, Grace. It is the way of life. We are born, and have to leave again. I am tired of this world, weary to the very centre of my soul. I long to be at peace and with your father again."

"I know, Mum. I do understand, and wherever he is, he will be waiting for you."

"You believe that too, dear?"

"I do," Grace said with certainty. "He will be waiting for you, Mum."

She gave her mother a kiss on the lips, and whispered, "From Dad, Mum. He sends you his love."

"Then I can go to sleep with peace in my heart. Oh! The blessed peace, no more pain either in body or soul."

Jane tiptoed in, with the coffee and a small plate holding four white tablets.

"Here you are, madam. Take these with your coffee, they will make you sleep."

"Thank you, Jane. You are a dear, true friend."

Grace helped her mother take the tablets. "What are they, Mum?"

"Morphine, the only thing that helps with my pain. In a few minutes, I shall be asleep. You go downstairs, and finish that excellent lunch with Jane. Drink another glass of wine, for me and your father."

Jane took her hand. "Sleep peacefully, madam. May God be with you."

"Go, Jane, take Grace with you. Be as good a friend to her as you have been to me."

"I will, madam." Tears were streaming down her face, as she put her arm around Grace's shoulders, and walked her out of the room.

Later that day, Anna passed into a coma, and two days later, she died peacefully in her sleep.

Grace, though devastated by the suddenness of her mother's death was, at the same time, relieved.

Anna had gone to her beloved husband.

Grace went down to the kitchen, where Jane stood tearfully stirring the ingredients for a cake. "Madam's recipes." She pointed to a notebook. "Her gift to us, to enjoy. Dear, dear madam, how I shall miss her."

"Me too, Jane. You will stay on, won't you, to look after the house, for I shall be travelling?"

"Where will you be going to, miss?"

"To Vienna. To the Convent of Santa Maria. I want to visit a nun there."

"You will be coming back?" Jane stopped stirring to look at Grace.

"I will be back later, Jane, and when I do, I want you to have another cake ready for me. For then I shall not be leaving again."

"That I will do, with pleasure. You just tell me when and I will have it ready." Jane stopped stirring, then lifted the spoon from the mixture and scraped it with her finger before putting it in the sink.

Chapter 18

Two weeks after the funeral of her mother, Grace flew to Vienna, taking only a small overnight bag with her. The address of the convent was in her shoulder bag. She hoped that she would not be too late, that Sarah would still be alive. When she arrived at Vienna airport, she hired a taxi to take her to the Gustavo, a small inner-city hotel, where she had booked a room.

Vienna, the city of music and art. If the purpose of her visit turned out all right, she would try to see as much as she could of it, but for the moment, however much she tried, she found it impossible to relax, in spite of its beauty.

"How long will you be staying?" the concierge asked, looking at her meagre hand luggage.

Grace looked around her. The little hotel was quite modern. There was steel and glass everywhere, with modern framed pictures of local scenes on the walls. "I am not sure. If I book the room for three days to start with, and then extend it if I need to stay any longer, would that be all right?"

The concierge gave her a crooked smile, then took a set of keys from the pegboard behind the desk. "That will be fine, Miss Brown. We are not fully booked at the moment." He handed her the room keys. "It is still early in the season, but next week we will be busy," he said with a flourish of his hands. "The town will be full of music lovers from all over the world. Herr Ingham, the famous young composer, is having his opening night at the Vienna Festival Hall in ten days' time."

"Ingham? Do you mean Frederic Ingham? I did not know he was here. Do you think there is a chance I might get a ticket to his concert?"

"Impossible, Miss Brown. The tickets have been sold out for the last two months. I am sorry if that is why you are here; you will be disappointed."

"No, that is not why I came. I knew Frederic Ingham as a child, but have long since lost touch with him and his family after they moved to South Africa. I shall be sorry to miss his concert, though."

"You can always buy his album. The shops are full of them."

"I might just do that, thank you." Grace started to walk towards the bright blue carpeted stairs.

"There is a lift, miss, to the right."

"It's all right, I will walk up, do me good after the flight. Oh! By the way, how do I get to the Convent of Santa Maria on the Rutastrasse?"

"That is easy. If you take a taxi, it should not be more than a ten-minute drive. The taxi stand is outside the bus station just down the road. If you prefer to walk, follow the road straight ahead, and when you come to

St Mary's Church in the main square, turn left, and just a short way down the road, you will see the convent."

"Thank you. I think I will walk; it is such a lovely day."

"So it is, Miss Brown. Enjoy it. Vienna is a beautiful city. I hope you will have time to do some sightseeing now that you are here."

"So do I." Grace went up to unpack then hung the one dress she had brought with her in the wardrobe. Her room was well furnished, with a dark wood writing desk and chair. Above the desk hung a beautiful antique gilt mirror. She opened the window and looked down at the busy street, then kicked her high heels off, put on a pair of flat walking shoes and tied a scarf around her head. She was ready to set out towards the convent.

Shoppers were everywhere, and children in bright clothes, with satchels on their backs. Their happy voices filled the air with joy.

Half an hour later, she stood in front of a high, yellow brick wall, surrounding a fifteenth-century building. The huge door, set into the wall, had an old-fashioned bellpull, which rang three times as she tugged it.

After a few minutes, a small window opened in the wall, and a white-capped nun's head appeared.

"How may I help you?" she inquired in a soft melodic voice.

"I have come to see Sister Teresa."

The nun's head disappeared, then the door started to open.

"Come in! Come in! My name is Sister Bernadette; I am assistant to the Reverend Mother. Who may I say is calling?"

"Grace Brown."

"A lovely name for a lovely young girl." Sister Bernadette smiled. "Reverend Mother did say you would be coming... from England, I believe?"

"That is right, Sister."

"I will go and see if Sister Teresa is up. She rests a lot and gets a little confused at times, but otherwise she is quite well. Please sit down." She pointed to a straight-backed wooden chair standing against the wall.

Grace's heart was pounding with nervousness. She took a deep breath, then closed her eyes.

"Follow me, my dear." Sister Bernadette was back. "Sister Teresa is looking forward to seeing you."

At the end of another corridor, they came to a small door. The sister knocked three times. She smiled broadly at Grace. "Here, we do everything by the three; Father, Son and Holy Spirit."

"I see what you mean, Sister," Grace managed to say through her dry lips.

A thin, high-pitched voice called from within. "Come in. Come in..."

Sister Bernadette gently pushed Grace in. "Here she is, Sister Teresa," she said cheerfully, before quietly closing the door behind her.

Grace stood still just inside the door, looking at the nun, sitting in a high back wooden chair, counting the beads of her rosary. Her face was pale, almost translucent, with high, prominent cheekbones and an unusually high forehead.

For a moment, neither of them spoke. Sister Teresa's intelligent eyes, so like those of Grace's father, looked curiously at the tall, slim woman, standing before her as still as a statue. Her mouth, beautifully formed and almost like that of a young girl, opened, as if she were about to say something, then closed again. Her age was difficult to tell, she could be anything between sixty and seventy, but later, when Grace had returned to her hotel, she worked it out that she was seventy-two years old.

Life had been less than kind to Sister Teresa. There were deep lines on her tired face and a constant frown across her eyes. Her fingers were long and slim. With a shock, Grace recognised them to be the same as her deceased father's. Curiously, she watched as Sister Teresa began to intensely stroke the crucified Christ, hanging from her rosary.

"Such a lovely surprise." She spoke slowly. "But who are you, my dear? I get the feeling we know each other?"

Her eyes scrutinized Grace. "You remind me of someone, but I don't seem to remember who."

"My name is Grace Brown, Sister Teresa. I found your journal amongst my father's papers after he died.

His name was Harry. I believe that he was your... and Adolph Hitler's son?"

Grace managed to get all the words out the way she planned, after having spent weeks in front of a mirror, practising. Her throat felt like dried parchment.

"May I take a glass of water?" She pointed to the carafe standing on a small table next to where Sister Teresa sat.

Sister Teresa went deadly pale, then bent her head gracefully.

"Harry," she whispered. "My little Harry's dead! When did it happen? My sweet little boy!" Tears welled up in her eyes and ran unashamedly down her wrinkled cheeks, whilst her fingers dropped the Christ.

"Seven years ago, Sister."

"My dear son, whom I was not allowed to keep. And you are his daughter. Did you say your name is Grace?"

"Yes, Sister." Looking at her, Grace felt sorry for the abrupt way she had spoken.

"Grace! Yes, that is a name my Harry would choose." She wiped her eyes with a tissue from a nearby box and blew her nose delicately, before putting the tissue into her pocket. Then she seemed to collapse in her chair.

"Sister Teresa!" Grace ran to her side. "I am so sorry, I should have prepared you for our meeting, but to tell you the truth, I was not sure if I could go through with it. It has been a shock to me after all these years...

to have discovered that I had a grandmother, not to mention who my grandfather was."

Sister Teresa began shaking her head from side to side, then fingered her rosary vigorously.

Grace sat down on a small footstool at her feet.

"Are you sure you are all right?" she asked, concerned. "Do you want me to call someone?"

"I will be all right in a moment." Sister Teresa smiled weakly. "What a life I managed to make for myself. Thrown out of my own family, denied my religion, and forced to live with a religious creed I did not understand. I even had to change my name!"

"I know, Sister Teresa. I have read your journal." Grace's voice was unusually sharp. She then stood up, turning her back to the sister, and walked over to look out of a small window, facing what looked like a vegetable garden, where two nuns in black and white habits were hard at work.

"I came to see if there is anything else you can tell me."

"All because of my love for a wonderful man." Sister Teresa reminisced in a soft voice.

"Please, Sister." Grace stopped her. "If we are thinking about the same Adolph Hitler." She held her hand up. "He was not a wonderful man." She emphasized the word "wonderful". "He was a monster, an evil monster, who was responsible for the most devastating atrocities any human being in history has ever done to mankind. And did you know that the one you call a wonderful man, deliberately had his henchmen, the Nazis, capturing and torturing my father's kind adoptive parents, before killing them? A monster, I tell you."

Grace continued, raising her voice. "And how did they find him? I will tell you: they followed the kind gardener whom you had given your documents to, when he delivered them to their home. After his adoptive parents had read the papers, they phoned my father, who was in France at the time, to tell him about them, and also about you. They told him where they would hide the papers, should anything happen to them.

"Something did happen to them. Do you know why they were tortured? Because they would not tell them where my father was. Your wonderful lover had sent the Nazis to find and kill him. His own son! That is how wonderful he was. My father decided to visit you, in spite of the danger involved. He, himself, told me what a pious woman you were, which I am not in a position to dispute."

Sister Teresa sat still, working the rosary beads, then pulled the wooden stool closer to her. "Come and sit down, Grace."

Grace went and sat down again, her face as hard as a stone.

"No, my dear, not a monster, but a strange lost soul, who throughout his young life was abused, misunderstood, and denied the chance to develop his great gift as a painter."

Grace gave her a look of disbelief.

"Oh yes, my dear! He would have been a great painter, given the chance. I have one of his paintings here. Would you like to see it?"

Before Grace had the chance to say anything, Sister Teresa had got up and crossed the room to withdraw the painting from her wardrobe.

Grace looked astonished. The painting, a soft green landscape with rivers flowing through it, was of such exquisite beauty, that it took her breath away. The light coming from the rising sun was of a colour she had never seen before. Its power was overwhelming.

There was just one figure in the painting, a small child. It was hard to say whether the child was a boy or girl, but the child was illuminated with light of an almost hypnotic power, leaving Grace unable to believe that such beauty could come from such a man as Hitler.

"Adolph painted this for me when I told him I was pregnant. It was still wet when he gave it to me. He assured me that one day he would be famous, one way or another, and rich. I believed him; he had such a wonderful gift."

Sister Teresa put the painting back in the wardrobe, and then sat down with a sigh. "Now why would you come here and take away all my wonderful memories of him?" She whimpered as she touched Grace gently.

"I am sorry, Sister Teresa. I have been cruel, but sometimes we have to face reality. Please forgive me, I will leave now so that you can rest."

"No dear, don't go yet. Just give me a minute to compose myself. I would like you to hear about Adolph's life."

"I am not sure I want to hear any more."

"I think you should. Like you said, sometimes we have to face reality, however unpleasant." Sister Teresa closed her eyes, as if in pain.

"Life was too cruel to him. He was hated and beaten by his half-brother and father. They even beat up his mother for protecting him. He was made to watch whilst they tied her to a chair and beat her with a belt. What do you think that would do to a small child's mind? He never got over the guilt, blamed himself for what they did to her. His half-brother was a bad lot, too; he ended up in prison.

"Adolph was treated worse than an animal, a lonely, unloved, starving little child, crying and praying for the evil in his house to stop, but it never did until that blessed day when his father died. He told me that was one of the happiest days in his life. Then finally he spent a few years with his mother, whom he did have some love for, before she, too, was taken from him by cancer. He told me how he sat beside her for two days without any sleep or food. He even did a painting of her on her death bed, willing her to come back to life… to change his life.

"There was no money. Even the house where they lived was repossessed, which left Adolph on the street to care for himself. He tried to sell his postcard paintings in the restaurants, but they laughed at him, and he was thrown out, even spat on. It seemed that whatever he turned to, failed.

"That was the time when he found himself with the rest of the city dropouts in the doss house. The council found him a job shovelling snow for the winter, but having no proper clothes, he became ill, as you will know from my journal.

"Adolph was denied the most fundamental issue of life, that of being truly loved. That was until he met me. We fell in love. For the first time, he had someone in his life whom he could love and who returned his love; someone to care for, as I cared for him. Someone who was prepared to give everything up for him, and then, that was also taken from him. Even his unborn child, whom he loved and continually talked about during the short time we had together… and that he was never to see.

"The painting was for our child, boy or girl; he painted the child so that it could be seen as either. He was beaten and thrown in prison, charged with influencing a young girl to steal. The prison officers nearly beat him to death. When he finally left the prison, his mind was twisted, and his whole being bent on destruction. Years later, he searched for the ones who had personally done him an injury, then had them and their families tortured and shot.

"I heard that, during the war, he went back to the prison and personally shot all the guards there. His mind by that time was poisoned with an uncontrollable hatred. A madness, that had no end, for you see, he was not afraid of dying… he was in a way already dead!"

Sister Teresa stopped talking and took a sip of water from a delicate glass standing next to a pale green carafe on her table.

"Where did you get all that information from?" Grace could barely get the words out.

"Elenora, my childhood friend, kept in touch with me by letter for a few years and also visited on two occasions. My parents had disclosed to her parents where they had sent me and also where they had sent poor Harry. After my parents were killed, they decided to tell her where I was.

"She, herself, became a victim of the holocaust in the last months of the war. News of her death was brought to me by her son, who survived. Though my heart cried for the millions that perished, I also cried for the only one I had ever loved." She pointed to the crucifix hanging above her bed. "Here we are taught to believe in God. To believe in his goodness and trust in his ways. Sadly, I do not find, however much I try, that I can believe any of it. I am here because I am forced to stay. Or at least I was. Now I am too old and tired to care about it."

Grace stood up. "Thank you for sharing your thoughts with me. I have tried to understand, and see things as you see them, but sadly I can't. Have you any idea how many children there are in the world, who are abused throughout their childhood, who are denied opportunities open to others, who go hungry and misunderstood on our streets today? But they don't turn into monsters… they don't try to eliminate a whole nation of people: they don't traumatize and rape or throw living, screaming children into open flames.

"They don't resolve to torture because their hearts and souls are full of pain. Frankly, I find it impossible to imagine that the man you describe in such a romantic way has any connection to me. God help me! How can I ever get married, have children, without fearing that they might turn out like him? You know what he has done, that wonderful man you speak so beautifully of? He has destroyed my life, too. I can never forgive him. Oh, my God! Why? Why?" She sobbed, bending almost double, in pain.

"My dear, I can understand your anger. It took years before I came to terms with mine. But try to understand. That last evil, that of our separation, was the final straw for him. His mind went. There was nothing more to live for, only a poisoned desire to make others experience the same pain as he had. A need to destroy, as his life had been destroyed. Such a terrible waste! Were we to have had a normal life together, history would have been rewritten."

Grace sniffed and then blew her nose. "Perhaps, Sister Teresa."

"But are we really in control of our destinies, or are we just a tool in the hand of something more powerful than ourselves?" Sister Teresa sighed. "Perhaps I shall find out soon."

"I don't know any longer what I believe." Grace dabbed her eyes where stinging tears threatened to ruin her carefully made-up eyes. "But I have to believe in something good, something noble, something worth living for, otherwise, my life would be pointless, too."

"I have to believe, Sister Teresa, that in each and every one, there is something honest and good, something we can trust and believe in."

"Grace, my dear grandchild. Such a beautiful girl and name, and in so many ways, like my beloved Harry, especially your eyes. Not even I could have chosen a better name for you. What can I say to you? I knew and loved a young man, who was to me the dearest person you could meet. The love he showed me was overwhelming. I remember, once, he brought me an ordinary flat stone about the size of a small dessert plate. On it, he had written the most beautiful poem for our unborn child. Sadly, it has since been lost, but I still remember the words. Listen…

To my darling
My room is filled with heavy scent,
the sweetness in the air,
the flowers look so fresh.
How many times we feel regret,
how openly we deny
the little choice we never get,

strength and courage of our voice.

But, like the heavy scent of flowers
that fills my room today,
your love will stay
and fill the air
throughout my lonely hour.

"He even found a single Christmas Rose and laid it next to the poem for me. Even without money and means, he found ways to show his love. And yet I also saw how, from one moment to the next, that love turned into a hellfire of hatred, bent on nothing but destruction without mercy or pity.

"My dear, he was no longer human, but had become what you so rightly describe — a monster. That is what humans have the power to do to each other. What a terrible waste of life, of all our lives…

"I have been denied my birthright, my family, and my religion, because of love. Love to destroy the one person I loved, turning him into an evil beast who, in turn, destroyed the lives of millions.

"Yes, my dear! I am not blind or deaf, nor do I live in denial of what happened. All I say again is that it would never have happened if we had been able to stay together. Never!" she repeated firmly.

"But the one good thing that I can tell you, Grace, is that after my parents died, their last will and testament was found. It had been made years before, and left me their total estate, which is quite substantial. My parents had great wealth. It is at the moment being held in trust.

"That, my dear, will be the only gift I can leave you. I had intended to leave it to the convent, but now that you, my only granddaughter, have come into my life, I shall see the solicitors about changing it, and make you, my heir. All I ask of you, is that you can find it in your heart to come once in a while for a visit, so that we might get to know each other a little better.

"Before you go, if you will be so kind as to write your full name and address down for me, so that I can make the arrangements for the will to be changed as soon as possible." She opened a drawer in the table and brought out a writing block and pen. "It will give me great peace of mind to know that my beloved child will live on in you and that part of him will be back in his rightful place."

Grace did as instructed, then asked to be excused. She could barely control her tears. She was not sure if she was crying for Sister Teresa, herself, or humanity. All she knew was that she had to get out.

"Sister Teresa, I will come again before going back to London." She gave her a kiss, uttered, "God be with you, Grandmother!" then quickly left the room.

She had only just closed the door, when her grandmother called her back.

"Grace, dear, come back for a moment. I feel there is more to be cleared up between us."

Grace reluctantly went back in.

"Grandmother, I am very tired. I have had a long and emotional journey here today."

"I know, dear. I am tired myself. But what I have to say can't wait, as I don't know how long I shall be here; my health and mind are not strong any more. But let me tell you, Grace, in spite of what I said before, part of me does believe in a supreme God. A God of mercy! A God of divine love! I pray that the..." Tears ran down her cheeks. "I pray that... no! Let us face the truth. I pray that love and goodness, will override evil... that the heart and soul of man will learn about compassion, about goodness. I pray that mankind will find it in their hearts to forgive, for only by forgiveness can they truly be free. All nations struggle against their individual powers, controlled by a handful of people at the top, for their own benefit. I have nothing more to say, for it has been said many times before.

"My parents perished in the most cruel and devastating circumstances, together with all our staff, on direct instructions from Adolph, who, God forgive him, tortured my father to get him to tell him where I was. My mother's back was broken by having a heavy staff deliberately driven into her. She died in agony, before being thrown into the furnace."

"My mother's family perished, too." Grace spoke quietly. "My two uncles, their wives and children. My mother never mentioned them again. All wiped out by the betrayal of one man, a friend of the family who believed in the madness of Hitler. My mother survived because she was in America at the time.

"My father's adoptive parents, as I said before, were also taken to the camps at the beginning of the war. My father, God help me, the son of that evil monster, was in France at the time visiting some gentile friends. That saved him. But why have you called me back to go over that again? We both know what he did!"

"Grace, the reason I called you back is to tell you that he was not responsible for his actions."

"Please, Grandmother, I am not a psychologist. I don't want to listen to this."

"Sit down, Grace." Sister Teresa's voice was firm. "You came here for a specific reason… to learn the truth. Now I will tell you. Adolph was not responsible for his actions. He was a pawn in the hands of a very clever German government that wanted a scapegoat who could do their dirty business for them, so that they were covered should the operation go wrong. It was not Hitler who wanted to get rid of the Jews, it was the German government. And it was not Hitler who decided on the concentration camps, but Herr Goering. The Jews had for many years been the controlling force behind the financial world market, and only by destroying them would they themselves be in power.

"The Germans had another motive. They did not want to conquer Europe, but Russia. Europe was just a stepping stone to get at Russia's mineral resources, such as gas and especially oil, of which Germany had none.

If they had succeeded with their dirty plan, it would have made Germany the world's strongest industrial nation, giving them enormous power and riches.

"After Adolph's initial beating at the police station, he was called into the chief of police's office, where he was asked to sit down. In the room were four other men, in civilian clothes. He never disclosed who they were."

"The Chief of Police opened a file in front of him, then said, 'I understand your fight is primarily with the Jews. There are Jews all over the world. How are you going to eliminate them all?'

"Even if Adolph had been able to speak, he made no answer, just sat looking down as blood ran from his broken nose and jaw onto the floor where it made a small puddle at his feet. He put his boots in the puddle and smeared it around. The chief went on, 'There are two ways to go about it. When you leave here, you can go out there' — he pointed towards the busy road — 'to kill as many Jews as you can before we catch you again, and when we do, that will be the end of you, too. The other way is for you to work as our agent and follow our instructions implicitly. You will be called the Führer, and as instructed by us, will be in control of eliminating all known Jews.

'You will have unlimited powers, again through our instructions, to invade Europe following a trail through Denmark into Norway, Great Britain, France, and then finally the coup de grace, Russia. Which is really, apart from the financial market, the only one we are interested in. The whole world will know you. You will be world-famous, you will be hated and despised and your name will be filth. But you will have the powers to eliminate any person of Jewish descent in any way you want. Are you interested?'

"Adolph nodded silently, still looking down. Then, through his swollen, bloodied lips, managed to ask, 'What are the chances of survival?'

'None, I am afraid, but hopefully your demise will not be before Germany has gained power over Europe and Russia.'

'What are my benefits from this?'

'To eliminate the Jews, steal their possessions, their precious art collections. Isn't that what you have always wanted to do? For as long as it lasts, you will be rich... rich beyond imagination.'

'You don't seem to give me much choice.'

'Good! Then when you have recovered from your small mishap.' He smiled. 'You will be sent over the border into Germany, where you will join the army and learn to handle a gun. After the initial six months of training, we will meet again, and from then on, you will follow our' — he pointed to the other men in the room — 'instructions to the letter. Is that understood? Should you have second thoughts about this, I am afraid we cannot let you go free, as you know too much.'

"Adolph was locked up in a secure cell where he had constant medical treatment, excellent food brought in from outside, books and games, in fact anything he wanted. He asked for paint and papers then asked permission to paint a picture for a friend, which was given.

"Adolph wrote down everything he had been told on the back of a large piece of paper, then carefully glued the edges together with another, which he painted on. The painting was delivered to Elenora, whom he had met once before, with me, with instructions to give it to me, should she find me.

"She brought it to me, and it did not take me long to discover the writing between the papers. Let me see if I can quote some of it… yes, he wrote:

My dearest love,

I hope this will reach you as it will be the only, and probably, the last letter you will receive from me.

He started by writing down what I have just told you, and then went on…

I must leave at once for Germany and will not be returning again, but remember, whatever you hear about me, one thing is true. I love you.

I am going to be a guinea pig for a new drug, which will be injected into me every day in high doses. The drug is meant to be able to control my mind, so that I will have no conscience about the work I am to carry out.

The state of my mind will be monitored daily, as will the minds of a close group of men under my command, who will also be injected with the same drug, but in smaller doses.

"Listen to this, Grace, these were his words too…

When weeds grow taller than the beautiful flower, then even that is overshadowed. Not dead, just overshadowed.
But weeds grow with a poisoned speed. Consuming everything within.

"Beautiful words from a beautiful soul, destroyed by man's devastating inventions — destroyed, I tell you!" Sister Teresa shook her head violently. "The hatred… so much hatred brought out from within. How, my dear, is it possible to survive?" She reached out for Grace's hand before continuing.

"Madness! An illness or a mind controlled by drugs! Who can say, except the people involved? All I can say again is I knew and was part of, for just a few wonderful months, a different person… a very different human being, who allowed himself to be used and manipulated, into the mentally distorted human being he was to become.

"On her last visit to me, Elenora told me a devastating story about the Nazis and what they did to Dr Möller and his family. It is a wonder I have stayed sane. Helen Möller was one of her friends, whose husband is… or rather was, a scientist who died by his own hand. Elenora's husband and Dr Möller had worked together for a number of years.

"Dr Möller had discovered a drug, of which just one-hundredth part of a grain would turn the human mind into that of a sadistic monster. Before the war, experiments with the drugs were carried out on long-term prisoners. They all turned into controlled human monsters. They were subsequently eliminated by lethal injection. Hitler, when he came out of prison, was sent away to be experimented on by Dr Möller, who was now working for the Secret Service in Germany. A strategy was organized to gain control over all the countries in Europe and Russia, and Hitler volunteered to be the leader of that.

"So you see, Grace, the story is parallel to what Adolph wrote to me. He always longed to be heard and seen, and here was his chance. He willingly agreed to be injected with the drug every day, after arriving in Germany for his leadership training. The end result, we both know. But what we do not know is that all the high-powered Nazis were also being experimented on, with the same drug. You must understand that without it, no man, or even God, could have made them do what they did.

"Elenora's husband died when he refused to co-operate after seeing the effect the drug had. The Nazis took their two youngest children, Claus, a boy of nearly five and Tammy, a darling little girl, and tortured them in front of him to make him co-operate.

"He nearly went mad, listening to their screams and pleadings as they were repeatedly raped and burned. Both children died from their injuries, and he himself took a poison pill, but not before shouting, 'May God curse you in all eternity, and may he grant me mercy for being the inventor of and party to such evil!' Then he fell down and died. But by then, it was too late. The Nazis confiscated everything in his laboratory and no doubt coerced others to carry on producing the drug.

"When Elenora came to see me the next day and told me the story, she also said that she herself had finished with living. If the Nazis had not picked her up the next day, I know she would have cut her life short herself. What had she to live for?

"So you see, Grace, I am not blind to what has happened, in spite of having lived here all these years. But my dearest dear, drugs are man's creation. Not God's! And with such evil, man has been able, for reasons unknown to us, or at least to me who knows nothing of world politics, to use these drugs to manipulate the minds of damaged or weak souls, such as your grandfather had. As I said before, had he been allowed to live a normal life with a loving wife and children, then history would have looked very different.

"Having said that, perhaps that is not so, for there will always be another damaged soul ready to play that monopoly, however devastating the effect might be. I make no excuses for his actions, but deep in my heart, I knew what a man he was, before that dreadful drug became his daily diet. He was then just another hard-done-by youth, trying to find his place in the world.

"I blame myself totally. Had I not agreed to elope with him, stealing from my parents, then none of this would have taken place. I alone am to blame. I live my life every day with a piercing pain of guilt. I blame my parents too, though they played a terrible price themselves for not allowing us to be together. They lived by their principles… honour, and belief, justified by what they thought of as rightful actions. How little we know. We act out of our own narrow-mindedness, our own desire not to lose face in the society where we find ourselves. But in doing so, we often lose what we most care for, and so destroy the very bonds that link us together.

"I am tired, my dear. Would you mind going now? Remember me in your prayers, and try to find it in your heart to forgive… and love me!"

Grace stood up to go, then turned around again. "I will. Oh! Grandmother, I nearly forgot, I have brought you a photograph of my father and mother and me at my first ball. I would like you to have it, together with these three volumes of father's poems. I think that you will find that many of his poems refer to the love he had for you. When I first read them, I never fully understood what he was saying. Now I know."

"I shall treasure them, my dear. Thank you for bringing them. I don't deserve so much kindness. Go now, for I am completely overcome. And I must rest."

"Goodnight, Grandmother — I will see you again."

"I hope so, God willing. Oh, Grace! You might also take these papers with you." Sister Teresa handed her a roll of papers tied with string. "They tell a story about another human being destroyed by the same drug. Read it one day, and it will prove what I have told you."

Grace took the tight roll of paper and put it into her bag, before silently closing the door behind her.

Chapter 19

Sister Bernadette walked towards Grace. She looked at her tear-stained face with a concerned frown.

"Are you all right, dear? Can I get you a glass of water? You look about to faint."

Grace shook her head.

"If you are sure, then I will let you out." The sister took her arm and walked her towards the exit. "It is never easy to say goodbye to someone we love," she said gently. "But do try to come again."

"I will, Sister, and thank you… Sister Bernadette, may I ask a favour? May I go to the chapel for half an hour before I leave?"

"But my dear, yes, of course! There should be no one there at the moment. Come with me."

They walked towards the far end of a long corridor, before stopping in front of the door leading into the chapel. Sister Bernadette smiled. "I will leave you here. When you are ready to go, just press that button." She pointed to it by the door. "Then I will come for you."

Grace sat down facing the simple altar, where a single white flower stood in a silver vase, next to a statue of the virgin mother, whose smile was as sweet as the scent coming from the flower. *I envy you,* she thought, looking at the Madonna. *You found something worth living for, and now, two thousand years later, you still, with your love and compassion, help millions of people to go on. If only I could find such a faith...*

From her bag she took the roll of paper her grandmother had given her. *I'd better read them, and then finish with it, so I can go on with my life.* She began reading the strong and bold handwriting.

I write this in haste, as I am preparing to go. I will send these documents to you via Johan the gardener. By the time you have read them, it will be all over for me. The blame for the catastrophic situation we all find ourselves in, is not yours, but that of the so-called rulers of our once beautiful country.

Enough! We have no more time to go over old ground; perhaps we are all to blame. Among my beloved Fritz's papers, I have found yet another paper on the experiments on children born in the camp. And... no, I can't talk about it, but will let you read it for yourself, so that you will understand the minds of those whose names we will never know.

I bless you and thank you for your friendship throughout my life. May God forgive us all.

Your loving friend, Elenora Roan.

Grace unrolled more papers.

Documents written by Doctor Roan.

As a scientist, we, that is my colleague and I, have created a monster we can no longer control. I hope and pray that in time it will not be used to destroy all mankind. Drugs such as these were used experimentally on various individuals, to test their effect on controlling the mind. Adolph Hitler was given one such cocktail every day, which clearly demonstrates how destructive and dangerous it is when being taken regularly and in large doses, such as were given to him.

Another experiment took place, which I was part of. Hitler was made to father a child by a beautiful Polish Jewess, as an experiment to see if the drug he was given would genetically be part of the child, and if so, to what extent it would be affected. The child's mother was eliminated after the birth.

Scientifically all very interesting, but with disastrous consequences.

The child I refer to was born a beautiful little girl. I, myself, tested her from birth until she was three years old. To my horror, I realized that her behaviour pattern was totally evil, her mind controlled by the drug to the same degree as was Hitler's.

The child, Baby X.1 on the official papers, was placed in the Führer's orphanage until three years old, then she was adopted by a German farming family, who were not to be told of her background. It was expected, as with most of the children born in the camp, that tests would be carried out on a regular basis, once a week to start with, followed by once a month. I would take fluid samples as well as doing physical analytical tests on her.

Baby X.1 had black hair, and deep, black-blue eyes, in a small cherub face. The child was exceptionally beautiful. Her adoptive parents were delighted with her, though they thought right from the start that her behaviour showed a great deal of aggression, which took the form of her biting and scratching them but, loving her as they did, they put it down to a strong will.

They called her Liza.

Dear God in Heaven, I don't think I can read any more. Grace laid the papers down on the bench next to her, then looked at the burning candles on the side stand. *Do I dare to burn them here?* The temptation was great.

No, I have to go through with this. Once I have read them all, I will destroy them, but not here in this holy place.

Then a voice spoke within her heart.

Sit down. You must read the rest of the papers, if only to prove that it was the drug administered daily to Hitler that turned him into the evil monster the world knows today. Your father, also Hitler's child, was a blessing to his adoptive parents, a normal, sensitive, talented child who grew up both wise and loving.

Grace wanted to interrupt her thoughts.

Silence, child! Let me continue. Come and sit down. Don't stand there with your hand on the doorknob as if you can't wait to get out.

Grace sat down again.

There are times in life when we have to face that which is unpleasant and disturbing, in order to find the inner peace we so desperately search for. Now pick up the papers and read on. The story has been written as it was documented, not eliminating any swear words, however vulgar.

Grace obediently picked the papers up, then began reading again.

Case 1
This is the unedited story of Baby X.1 (To be called Liza).

The morning had been still. None of the trees in the orchard surrounding the small farmhouse, were moving a single leaf. It was as if they were holding their breath, expecting something to happen.

Today was Liza's fifth birthday. She was warm and tucked up in bed with her favourite doll.

Liza had big blue eyes, a small, pert nose and black hair that curled naturally when wet. Her hands had unusually large fingers, and her long legs were complemented by dainty feet. Liza lived with her adoptive parents, Agate, a meek woman, and Hans, a farmer, on their small landstead, just outside Berlin, Germany.

Liza would have liked a brother or sister to play with, but her mother had told her that would not happen. So Liza would make believe that her doll was her little sister. She would dress it in clothes like her own, give it milk and comfort it when crying.

Liza was not a difficult child, apart from moments of violent tantrums when she would kick her doll, sending it flying across the room. This was one such day. She got out of bed, picked up the doll, then violently smashed its head on the floor.

"Serves you right, stupid doll, for not doing what I asked you to do." She kicked it again, then cried as she looked at the doll's broken head.

Agate came running in and, seeing the broken doll, thought it had been dropped.

She picked it up carefully whilst speaking in a comforting voice to Liza.

"Don't worry, darling, I will get some plasters and fix it for you. It might look like it is straight out of surgery, but you will love it just the same."

Liza kept on crying. When Agate went to comfort her, she bit her hand so hard that she drew blood.

"Liza, what is the matter with you? What did you bite me for?" Agate sucked on her hand to stop the blood from running down her arm. "Sometimes, I don't understand you, child. I will just have to do the best I can for you..."

She went out, closing the door.

"What does the stupid cow mean by that?" Liza said to herself. "I hate her. I hate everything." She threw the doll down again and kicked it. "Stupid doll, I am going to kill you, you stupid doll," she kept repeating.

Agate went to speak with her husband. Liza could hear their raised voices coming through the gaps in the floorboards.

"Perhaps we made a mistake," her mother began, "adopting a child from the camp. We don't know what kind of background she has come from. Liza's behaviour is most unpredictable. Whatever I do makes no difference when she has one of her turns."

"Stupid cow," Liza muttered again, as her mother's voice carried on.

"We will have to see what we can do about it. Perhaps Uncle George will be able to advise us? After all, he is the one who found the adoption agency for us."

"Adoption! What is that stupid woman talking about? I will ask Grandpa when he comes tonight. I hate his smelly old farts, and Grandma is always picking her nose before sitting down to eat. Disgusting old farts... I hate them, and one day I am really going to hurt them." Liza smiled to herself. "I will cut off their heads, like they do to the chickens. I will cut off their hair, and put sticks in their eyes, and hear them scream like this..." Liza gave an ear-piercing scream.

Her mother burst through the door.

"Liza, what is it now?" As she went to comfort her, Liza picked up a pencil from her table and stabbed it into the eye of her mother, who gave a great cry. That brought the father running. He looked at his wife, who had fainted, and Liza standing over her, grinning. He slapped her face hard, and shouted, "You monster! I

will have you locked up. What have we done, taking you into our house?"

Liza sneered at him, showing her sharp white teeth, before running over and opening the hot water tap in the sink, which quickly filled and then started to overflow.

Her father went to turn it off.

Liza, in the meantime, ran over and picked up the penknife he had dropped whilst helping Agate. She opened it, and plunged the knife repeatedly into his back. As he collapsed, dying, on the floor, she opened the hot tap again and watched as the steaming water ran down over the two mutilated bodies and the broken-headed doll.

She then ran, laughing, out of the room and over to the neighbours' house, banging on their door shouting, "Helga! Helga! My mum, my dad! Someone has killed them!" She began sobbing hysterically.

Helga opened the door, then shouted to her son, Peter. "Look after her, something has happened to Agate and Fritz." She ran across the courtyard, nearly tripping over a squawking hen that was trying to find shelter in the hen house, up the stairs and into the room, where the two bodies lay bleeding in the steaming water still pouring out of the sink. She quickly turned off the tap, then ran down to phone the police and a doctor.

Liza was having milk and biscuits in the kitchen when Helga returned home to look after her.

"My doll! My doll," she cried. "I want my doll!"

"Yes, dear. Don't worry, I will get it for you." Helga ran back to the house again, where the police and doctors were now busy.

"Could I have the little one's doll? She is crying for it," she asked the stern-looking police officer who was bending over the bodies.

"I am afraid not, madam. Its head is smashed and covered in blood. Where is the girl?" He looked at her with piercing, black eyes.

"In my kitchen."

"Good. Make sure you keep her there; we will be over to interview her in a few minutes."

On returning, Helga took the still sobbing child in her arms. "Don't worry a bit, my love, I will get you another doll."

And so Liza got a splendid new doll, complete with wardrobe.

Liza's father survived the attack and was able to tell the police what had happened. Agate died of shock due to her injuries.

Liza herself was placed in a locked ward in a mental institution, where she stayed until she died at the age of seventy-two.

Case 2

This is even more remarkable.

I had also been experimenting with a drug, which we would be injecting into young domestic animals such as cats and dogs, together with a sophisticated method of inserting a minute microchip into their brains. With such sophisticated and advanced technology built into it, the chip enabled us to monitor their thought processes... in short, reading their minds. The microchip was developed by a brilliant scientist, Dr Herman Jacobs, and me. We spent most of our adult lives working on this project before he, too, was taken to the camps for not allowing the Nazis access to his discovery.

They tried to convince him to develop it in such a way that it could be used for humans. I need not say what that would have led to.

For years before the war, it was known to the Secret Service within the government what we were working on. We were given generous allowances; in fact, the experiment was so successful that we were able to set up a retirement home for the animals too old to be of further use, though it did enable us to monitor the interaction between them.

We found that there was no difference in life span between our test animals and other, untreated animals. Most of them lived to the normal age of between eighteen and twenty-five years without any major ills. Occasionally we would give the animals to families with young children. In this way, we were able to see how they would differ from the ones kept in the laboratory.

This is just a brief background, so that the enclosed sample story will make sense to the reader.

The cat in the story was one of our first experiments and was given to a family with young children, where it stayed until their disastrous end during the war.

This is its story, monitored by us. We were able to trace the whereabouts of the cat, which had suffered great traumas. It was then placed in the retirement home.

<u>*The cat's story.*</u>

There was once a cat that willed itself blind, for it had no wish to see anything else. The cat, now in retirement, sat all day in its rocking chair, rocking back and forth, back and forth, in a rhythmic way. The other cats in the retirement home thought kindly of the old blind cat, and put Beethoven's Fifth Symphony on, so that it could rock in time to the music.

Back and forth, back and forth; I have seen it all; back and forth, back and forth; there is nothing more for me to see. Let me close my eyes to the horror and dream of happier times when I lived as a treasured pet, with my little master, Edward, and Charlotte, his twin sister, in a fine house leaning against an old crumbling wall... or was it the other way about?

The cat shook its head, trying to remember pale green fingers of fungus, which grew in profusion where young trees and blossom sprang forth from the frozen earth every spring. My life, *thought the blind cat*, was one of luxury. I even had a private doctor coming every week to examine me. I was petted and loved, *it sighed.*

Charlotte tied a red ribbon with a little bell around my neck that rang so beautifully every time I moved. The little birds I playfully tried to catch teased me by flying right in front of me. Every time I leapt for them, they swivelled in their flight just outside my reach.

Hunger was an unknown thing to me. I had my own little bowl painted with small birds in flight for both water and food. Every time I ate my food, I pretended to catch and eat them. I was never cold or wet, for I had my own bed shaped like a round pillow, where I was tucked in every night, though I much preferred to sleep close to the soft neck of Charlotte, who was then six years old and the most beautiful little girl anyone could imagine.

Charlotte's long blonde hair, smelling of summer fruit, was soft as silk, and as I put my nose close to her neck I could hear her pulse beating, one — two — three — four, I used to count the beats, but would then fall asleep. Sometimes, I would climb into Edward's bed next to Charlotte's, then creep under his blankets right down to his feet, where I would nip his toes, which made him wake up.

'Auk! You silly cat, come here!' Edward would then take me by the scruff of my neck and drag me up next to him, then lovingly put his arms around me, before going back to sleep.

I seem to remember, too, that there were days when I had my fur brushed endlessly. It seems to me that I could use some of that right now. It sighed, as it turned its head to bite off some of its matted fur balls, then gave up the attempt, as both its teeth and strength had gone. Tears ran silently down its furry cheeks as it remembered the horror that followed.

It was in the early morning at about three o'clock. Frost was in the air, making the tree outside the bedroom window stiff and white, as it reached its naked branches up towards the star-filled sky. Discarded branches lay on the ground, twisting and turning in the wind, spitting out bits of living wood before dying.

The stars patrolling the sky with their display of diamonds suddenly closed their doors. For a moment, the darkness seemed to cover everything, even the flowers in the garden lifted their sleepy heads, and then protectively covered them with their leaves.

The earthworm, up for a breath of air, hurriedly burrowed another trench and fast disappeared. Even the little birds that had not migrated covered their heads with their wings, as they sat, shaken, in their nests.

The old cat tried to stop the memories. It had no wish to remember anything else, but somehow the thoughts could not be silenced.

Oh! How I wished, it meowed… that somehow, I could blind my mind, too, for it is more terrifying than my sight.

What was it that had happened? The old blind cat could only describe it as if the still sky was suddenly filled with the most monstrous noise, so loud, that the whole house shook so violently that the pot plant on the window sill fell down with a crash. The children woke up, and started crying for their parents.

The children's parents were out at a wedding, and not expected back before the next day.

Emma, the au pair, came running in. She pulled down the blackout blind as the bombs began falling in the distance and the whining of Spitfire engines passed over the house.

"Go down into the cellar!" she shouted to them as she ran to phone their parents.

Edward ran over to the window and peeped out, watching as two planes were shooting at each other. One of them caught fire as the other exploded in a myriad of sparks. Debris fell, together with a parachute, silently towards the Earth, where it got caught up on the branches of the old tree.

The man strapped into the harness gestured to Edward to open the window, which he did. Having unstrapped his harness, he climbed into the room where he collapsed, gasping, on the floor.

Edward stood horrified, shouting for Emma and Charlotte.'

The old cat stopped rocking. Silently the other cats gathered around in a circle on the floor.

"Tell us, old cat, what happened next?"

The cat shook its head. "I can't," it whispered. "It will drive me mad."

"You are already mad!" whispered an old cat, stretching its arthritic back legs. "Perhaps, if you

speak, the madness will leave you, letting you die in peace."

"It is too late!"

The blind cat began rocking again, as Beethoven continued playing softly in the background. "What do you want me to tell you?" It licked its paws.

"Start at the beginning," they chorused.

"There was no beginning, only an end," it replied bitterly.

"The soldier took out his gun, then shot Edward and Charlotte. Emma tried to protect them as they screamed, falling into a pool of blood. The soldier hit her hard, then ripped her nightgown off before raping her, then took his knife and cut off her breasts, before shooting her too. For some reason unknown to me, he picked me up and put me under his tunic, stroking and petting me, calling me by a strange name. I hissed and spat, trying to claw my way out.

"He then unfastened my ribbon from around my neck and tied my paws together with it, before putting me into his large rucksack. Then he went into the kitchen, where he began searching the cupboards for food, stuffing his mouth with whatever he could find.

"A mouse ran across the tabletop, where it had enjoyed a few crumbs. He grabbed it and squeezed it with his hands until it died, then threw it into the rucksack for me to eat.

"Children, go to sleep," whispered the old blind cat. "I have nothing more to say."

The music stopped. The cats crept silently back to their beds, leaving the blind cat sitting rocking in its chair, back and forth, back and forth.

"Hitler's child, that's who he was."

"Hitler's child, that monster, that evil blond monster I first encountered on that beautiful frosty morning," it kept repeating, as it rocked, back and forth, back and forth.

There were numerous such incidences due to the experiments carried out with my drugs. Numerous such children were being born to the Nazis. I have kept the knowledge of my experiments away from my own family in order to protect them, should anything happen to me.

In truth it is only by manufacturing drugs that man can control man totally. The evil of man against man bears no resemblance to birth defects that can and will render a man unable to cope with life and his fellow men. We are talking about something much more powerful; a manufactured, controlled body of evil, used on man.

I will say no more, but only hope that man will, in time, be able to look around him with pride and joy at his achievement, instead of with the heart-rendering suffering poisoning my mind.

Let man treasure the freedom of beauty and love, as he travels peacefully on his journey. Let him understand about compassion. Let him learn to forgive, to rise up above the devastation and move forward into the light, which will, like a beacon, shine for those who have the courage to open the blinds in their hearts.

"Miss Grace! Miss Grace! Wake up, you are shaking all over. Are you sick?"

Grace opened her eyes and looked around her, bewildered. Sister Bernadette stood shaking her gently.

"I am so sorry, Sister, I must have fallen asleep."

"I think you must… you have been here for over two hours. We are about to come in for our evening prayers."

"I am so sorry," she repeated. "Will you see me out?"

"I will. Don't forget to take those with you." She pointed to the scattered papers on the floor.

Grace quickly gathered them up, then tightened her headscarf before following the sister towards the exit.

She felt emotionally drained and totally disorientated. All she knew was that she wanted to get away from the convent, from her grandmother, God forgive her, and get back to the safety of her hotel room as quickly as possible. She walked slowly as in a dream, then suddenly collided with a tall, elegantly dressed man.

"Hey there! Watch where you are going, young lady, you nearly tripped me up." He grabbed hold of her arm to steady himself, then looked closer at her in the soft street light. "Good God, it can't be! Grace?"

"It can't be you!" he repeated. "What are you doing here in Vienna?" Frederic looked at her tear-stained face. "Hey! You don't need to cry just because you tripped me up, it was not that bad," he said good-humouredly. "But Grace, you seem to be in a bad way, what has happened?"

"Not now, Frederic. I can't speak about it."

"I am so sorry. I don't like to see you looking so unhappy. Are you coming to the rehearsal of my concert tonight?"

Grace shook her head.

"All right, but don't let us lose touch with each other again. Can we go for dinner later? I want to tell you so many things about Mother and my life in South Africa. You know my father died last year?"

"Yes, I heard. I am so sorry. We haven't been in touch for some years, Frederic; I would like to have dinner with you later."

"Great, where are you staying?" Grace wrote down the address for him.

"Here, dry your tears." He gave her his handkerchief. "Keep it," he said as she handed it back to him. "You can give it back to me tonight. Grace, how extraordinary to bump into you here… you don't know how many times I have thought about you." He gave her a kiss on the cheek.

"Just a moment, Frederic." She gently pushed him away then walked towards a tramp, who was warming his hands over a small open fire burning in a brazier used for roasting chestnuts. She took out the crumpled papers from her handbag, then fed them to the flames.

"You are a good omen, miss." The tramp rubbed his hands as the flames rapidly devoured the papers. "I was just hoping someone would come along with something to burn. Does us both good, no doubt!"

"No doubt." She smiled, then took out ten Deutsche Marks. "Here... to warm the rest of you."

He gave her a toothless grin. "I will do that, miss. I will do that. As I said, a good omen!"

Grace returned his smile. *You have no idea how good...*

Frederic stood watching from a distance, and made no comment when she returned. He simply said, in a matter-of-fact manner, "It will be after ten o'clock before the concert finishes. I hope it will not be too late for you?"

"It will be perfect, Frederic."

"Good. See you then." Frederic started to go, then turned around. "Oh! By the way, Grace, do you still have that Bugatti?"

In spite of herself, she couldn't help laughing. "I will tell you tonight, silly!"

END